THE NEW PAUL AND
VIRGINIA

'Pessimism as to the essential dignity of man is one of the surest marks of the enervating influence of this dream of a celestial glory.'

Mr Frederic Harrison

THE NEW PAUL
AND VIRGINIA

or

Positivism on an Island

W. H. MALLOCK

Edited with an introduction by
JOHN D. MARGOLIS

UNIVERSITY OF NEBRASKA PRESS · LINCOLN

Publishers on the Plains

Introduction copyright © 1970 by the University of Nebraska Press

All rights reserved

Standard Book Number 8032–0711–5

Library of Congress Catalog Card Number 74–88087

Manufactured in the United States of America

CONTENTS

INTRODUCTION

THE intellectual controversies of the latter half of the nineteenth century were not taken lightly by the Victorians. While the rhetorical and philosophical excesses of many eminent Victorians seemed almost to invite the chastening treatment of satire, the polemical wars of the period were generally conducted with a passionate high seriousness. Such was the situation described by George Meredith in 1877:

You see Folly perpetually sliding into new

shapes in a society possessed of wealth and
leisure, with many whims, many strange ail-
ments and strange doctors. Plenty of common
sense is in the world to thrust her back when
she pretends to empire. But that first-born of
common sense, the vigilant Comic, which is
the genius of thoughtful laughter, which would
readily extinguish her at the outset, is not
serving as a public advocate.[1]

That very year, as if in answer to Meredith's challenge, a young man who had recently come down from Oxford published
The New Republic, a satire on prominent
Victorian thinkers which enjoyed immediate
success. When, the following year, he brought
out another novel in the same vein, *The
New Paul and Virginia,* readers had cause
to hope that the comic spirit had found a
powerful new voice in England. However,
W. H. Mallock was a creature of his age, and
he soon began to exercise his literary suasion

[1] "The Idea of Comedy, and of the Uses of the
Comic Spirit," *New Quarterly Magazine* 8 (1877), 23.

more directly through literary essays, didactic novels, and political and religious tracts. His later work has been justly forgotten. But the two satires, which seemed to Mallock merely preliminary to his proper mission as a Victorian sage, have earned him a small but secure place in Victorian literary history.

In a sense, the twenty-eight years before the publication of *The New Republic* had been a period of temperamental and literary preparation for his brief career as a satirist. Born in 1849 of an old West Country family, William Hurrell Mallock was the son of a cleric whose ill health and generous livings freed him from the performance of divine service. His mother was the daughter of Archdeacon Robert Hurrell Froude and a brother of James Anthony Froude and Richard Hurrell Froude; Mallock's middle name marked his Froude heritage of literary achievement and religious conscientiousness. Looking back from 1920 to the years of his childhood, Mallock could recognize that "the most remarkable feature of the period" was "a sequence of remarkable and momentous changes—changes alike in the domains of science, religion, and society."[2] In his early years, however, he had been comfortably isolated from those changes. The young Mallock never doubted the security of his family's aristocratic position; and his religious convictions were no less assured: "That the universe was created in the inside of a week four thousand and four years before the birth of Christ, and that every word of the Bible was supernaturally dictated to the writer, were to [him] facts as certain as the fact that . . . the date of the battle of Hastings was 1066" (p. 34). The most unconventional of Mallock's youthful attitudes were, perhaps, those towards literature. His tutors presented the poetry of Wordsworth and Tennyson as "mo-

[2] W. H. Mallock, *Memoirs of Life and Literature* (New York and London: Harper and Brothers, 1920), p. 2. Page numbers for other quotations from this source are given in the text.

dels of beauty and edification." But William demurred. Significantly, his tastes were more conservative. "Wordsworth I thought ridiculous," he recalled. "Tennyson seemed to me unmanly and mawkish." He preferred, instead, Dryden and Pope; and reading widely in the poetry and drama of the Restoration and eighteenth century, Mallock fancied himself "destined to accomplish a counterrevolution in the literary taste of England" (pp. 35, 37). As a youth he found even in the Sunday sermon an opportunity to exercise his harmless predilection for satire; but the more earnest attempts, of which he was vaguely aware, to discredit the Bible represented for him "a mood so blasphemous and absurd as not to be worthy of a serious man's attention" (p. 84).

The shock was great, then, when he went away to a tutor and later to Oxford and discovered that, in fact, the attention of many serious men was engaged by liberal social and theological thought. His tutor's suggestions that dissenters might enjoy salvation no less than Churchmen and that the sacraments were mere symbols were "shocking in an extreme degree." Faced with such theological liberalism, Mallock began asking himself the question (which—without ever coming to a conclusive answer—he asked throughout his life) "whether the Church of Rome was not perhaps the one true religion, after all" (p. 45).

At Oxford, Mallock found that the dons, like his tutor, assumed "that the dogmatic theology of the churches was as dead as the geocentric astronomy . . . . Their denials of everything which to me had been previously sacred appalled me like the overture to some approaching tragedy. Their confident attempts at some new scheme of affirmations affected me like a solemn farce" (p. 82). As a child, listening to the Sunday sermon, Mallock had felt the absurdity "of the arguments by which the orthodox clergy endeavored to defend doctrines which were then for myself indubitable." At the university

> I became conscious of an absurdity to which as a child I had been a stranger—namely, the absurdity of the arguments by which men who repudiated orthodoxy altogether endeavored to establish in its place some purely natural substitute, such as the 'enthusiasm of humanity'... In addition... [there] was the absurdity, common to all parties alike, of supposing that, if the cardinal doctrines of religious orthodoxy were discredited—namely, that the human soul is immortal, that the human will is free, and that a God exists who is interested in the fortunes of each soul individually—these doctrines, in disappearing, would take away with them nothing but themselves alone.

To Mallock it was clear that "unless the orthodox doctrines could be defended in such a way that in all their traditional strictness they could once more compel assent, life, in the higher sense of the word, would . . . soon cease to be tolerable" (p. 85).

Given his literary tastes and interests, it was natural that he should first have chosen satire for a means of such defense. In his second year at the university he began the composition of a book in which he hoped "to give a comprehensive picture of the moral and intellectual condition to which my Oxford experiences had by that time raised or reduced me" (p. 87). That book was *The New Republic*, at once the beginning and the apex of his public literary career. Modelled on the "conversation novels" of Thomas Love Peacock, *The New Republic* brings together at an English country house a group of guests who, as conscientious Victorians, pass their weekend asking "What is the aim of life?" Among those included in this *roman-à-clef* were figures representing Matthew Arnold, William Kingdon Clifford, Thomas Henry Huxley, Benjamin Jowett, Walter Pater, John Ruskin, and John Tyndall. In so diverse an assembly there was, naturally, lively disagreement regarding the aim of life, and much of the

comedy of the book issued from the juxta-
position of personalities and philosophies.
But in his first satiric novel, as in his second,
Mallock also made effective use of the *reduc-
tio ad absurdum,* pushing the arguments of
most of his philosophers "to some consequence more extreme, but more strictly logi-
cal, than any which those who proclaimed
them either realized or had the courage to
avow" (p. 88).

The New Republic was frequently reprinted and, apparently, widely read; yet its
critical reception was decidedly mixed. The
Contemporary Review spoke of "the extraordinary literary power of this little book."
But others were not so enthusiastic; their
reservations offer an interesting example of
Victorian literary taste and an anticipation
of the notices which would greet *The New
Paul and Virginia* a year later. The *Saturday
Review* found a "want of taste" in Mallock's
modelling his *New Republic* portraits on contemporary figures and, worse yet, in his hav-

ing capitalized on a "close observation of the daily habits and conversation of the subjects." (Since he had never met most of the men he satirized, this indictment testifies to Mallock's remarkable success in characterization.) Similarly, the *Athenaeum* expressed misgivings about the very conception of the book. "It does not need demonstration," the reviewer asserted, "that the parodist element is one which should be kept to its place, and that that place is a minor one." The *Athenaeum* reviewer was not amused. "A parody in two volumes is something of a monstrosity," he declared.[3]

Yet amusement was hardly Mallock's primary goal. Like all satire, *The New Republic* had a constructive purpose: it sought to demonstrate the preposterousness of the variety of heterodox Victorian philosophies in order to emphasize the necessity for a return to

[3] *Contemporary Review* 30 (1877), 1099; *Saturday Review*, 5 May 1877, pp. 554–555; *Athenaeum*, 24 March 1877, p. 378.

orthodoxy. Yet there was a still more personal motive behind Mallock's composition of his first novel. The mood to which his Oxford experience had brought him seemed "nothing better than a disease," and he had written the book to purge himself of that mood. "My hope," he said, "was that I should get rid of it by expressing it once for all as pungently and as completely as I could, after which I would address myself to the project of finding a foundation for some positive philosophy of life." The attempted purgation was apparently insufficient. "When ... *The New Republic* had been completed and given to the world, I felt that my sense of the absurdities of current liberal philosophy had not even yet exhausted itself; and I presently supplemented that work by another—*The New Paul and Virginia, or Positivism on an Island*" (pp. 89–90). Thus, *The New Paul and Virginia* is, in a sense, an appendix to *The New Republic.* Like its predecessor, it had its genesis in Mallock's dismay over Victorian

heterodoxy and like *The New Republic* it
implicitly argues man's need for guidance
from religious orthodoxy in the search for an
answer to the question, "What is the aim
of life?"

At the time Mallock was writing his satire
he was also gaining considerable attention
with a series of periodical essays which he
revised and collected in 1879 under the title
Is Life Worth Living? The essays endeavored
through Christian apologetics to address the
same situation that had concerned Mallock
in the satires. Contemporary reviews of the
collection and its frequent reprinting sug-
gest that Mallock enjoyed from it even greater
immediate success than from his satires. If
the Victorians felt uncomfortable with satire,
they were very much at home with religious
controversy. Today, however, it is difficult to
take Mallock's apologetics seriously. The
writing is verbose and saccharine; the arguments scarcely seem original after decades
of Victorian religious controversy; and his

understanding of the Roman Catholicism he defends seems no more clear than his understanding of the rationalism he attacks. Nevertheless, the essays are useful in establishing explicitly the concerns which were exercising Mallock in *The New Paul and Virginia*, the assumptions which lay behind that satire, and the cast of mind out of which such a book grew.

In the first of those essays, "Modern Atheism," Mallock pointed to the challenge posed by rationalism to Christian belief. And among the rationalists, scientists received special attention since "in the opinion of the world at large, it is the authority of men of science by which Unbelief has been established."[4] As he explained several months later, Mallock sought in his essays to point out the dangerous consequences of his age's doubt: "It is my aim to make [people] see what in these days we are really all debating about, and to

[4] "Modern Atheism: Its Attitude Towards Morality," *Contemporary Review* 29 (1877), 171.

show them that it is not only first causes, and natural selection, and the condition of the universe millions of years ago; but the tone and character of our human existence now— our hopes, our fears, our affections. . . ."[5] Only a sense of moral value can make life worth living, Mallock insisted, and the only possible source of such value is the God of Christianity. In their rationalist doubt of God, modern thinkers were denying the only possible foundation for the continued value of life. "To all moral life, Religion—a belief in God—is essential," Mallock wrote. "And . . . to all that gives our existence either zest or dignity, a belief in the moral life is essential."[6] In particular, one brief passage included in an essay published a few months before the appearance of *The New Paul and Virginia* suggests the judgment behind that satire:

[5] "Is Life Worth Living? (I)," *Nineteenth Century* 2 (1877), 252–253.

[6] "Faith and Verification," *Nineteenth Century* 4 (1878), 673.

> Our present school of moralists are men who would still retain the moral passion, but at the same time they deny the existence of its only possible object, and set up others that are utterly inadequate either to excite or to appease it. Such is the enthusiasm of humanity, which is now offered as an explanation of it. This is really nothing but the desire of God, which will not confess itself.[7]

In his essays he had used one approach to expose the inadequacy, indeed the absurdity, of that "present school of moralists." In *The New Paul and Virginia* he turned to satire. When it appeared, there was some uncertainty as to just which modern school of moralists was under attack. On its first publication in the *Contemporary Review* for April, 1878, it was titled "Positivism on an Island," and although this became the subtitle when it appeared in book form, the suggestion remained that *The New Paul and Virginia* concerned the Positivist teaching of Auguste

[7] "Is Life Worth Living? (II)," *Nineteenth Century* 3 (1878), 166.

Comte. It was understandable, then, that readers were confused when they found that Mallock's central satiric character was as much a Darwinian as a Comtean and that the satire drew more attention to the ideas of contemporary men of science than to those of figures associated with Comtean Positivism. But Mallock's satire was intentionally general. Whatever the specific disagreements of the moralists he treated, they shared a disbelief in a supernatural, non-empirical reality and confidently asserted that an adequate system of ethics could be based on purely rational foundations. Mallock's positivist Professor Paul Darnley was not uncomfortable borrowing at one moment from the ideas of Frederic Harrison and at the next from Harrison's frequent critic, Thomas Henry Huxley. Darnley's mind "was like a sea, into which the other great minds of the age discharged themselves, and in which all the slight discrepancies of the philosophy of the present century mingled together and formed one harmonious whole."

The eclecticism of the Darnley mind and the breadth of Mallock's satire were made clearer when, in July, 1878, *The New Paul and Virginia* was issued as a book. To the original text Mallock appended a collection of passages from the writings of five prominent Victorians. And in this primer of late nineteenth-century heresy he at once indicated some of the sources for his understanding of positivism and anticipated his readers' objections that he had misrepresented the positions of those he was satirizing.[8] Three scientists alluded to in *The New Paul and Virginia* had figured earlier in *The New Republic*. The appearance of William Kingdon Clifford, Thomas Henry Huxley and John

[8] Throughout this introduction "positivism" is used to refer to the general spirit of rationalism and empiricism current in nineteenth-century thought. The capitalized "Positivism" refers to the specific manifestations of that spirit based on the writings of Comte.

Tyndall in both satires indicates not only
Mallock's continued interest in these men,
but also their important positions in the
scientific and intellectual life of their time.
Had they been merely eminent scientists,
Clifford, Huxley, and Tyndall would have
been of less interest to Mallock as satiric tar-
gets, but each of them had gone beyond his
scientific role in publicly exploring the implications of science for religious belief. Tyndall
might well have been speaking for all three
when, in his famous Belfast Address to the
British Association in 1874, he proclaimed:
"The impregnable position of science may
be described in a few words. We claim, and
we shall wrest from theology, the entire domain of cosmological theory. All schemes and
systems which thus infringe upon the domain
of science must, in so far as they do this, sub-
mit to its control, and relinquish all thought
of controlling it."[9] What especially exercised

[9] *Fragments of Science* (2 vols.; New York: D. Appleton and Company, 1896), II, 197.

Mallock's satiric temper, however, was the insistence upon the possibility of man's continued experience of something akin to religious feeling founded on new secular bases.

While the scientists were generally either indifferent or antagonistic to the organized Positivist movement then developing in England, Frederic Harrison and Harriet Martineau, the two other writers cited in Mallock's notes, were closely associated with the Comtean philosophy. Shortly after the publication of *The New Paul and Virginia*, Harrison became president of the English Positivist Committee. And though Miss Martineau was never a complete, practicing Comtean, she had been closely linked with the movement through her popular abridged translation of Comte's *Positive Philosophy* (1853). In her preface she reflected the enthusiasm which inspired the Positivist movement during the latter half of the century:

If it be desired to extinguish presumption, to draw away from low aims, to fill life with worthy occupations and elevating pleasures, and to raise human hope and human effort to the highest attainable point, it seems to me that the best resource is the pursuit of Positive Philosophy, with its train of noble truths and irresistible inducements. The prospects it opens are boundless . . . .[10]

Their almost evangelical rationalism alone would have rendered Clifford, Harrison, Huxley, Martineau, and Tyndall appropriate "authorities" for Mallock's study of positivism. Yet four of the five—the four whom Mallock drew upon most frequently in the notes and in the text—were associated by an even closer bond. All but Martineau were members of that quintessentially Victorian institution, The Metaphysical Society, which had been organized in 1869 in the hope that out of reasoned discourse among eminent men of widely various persuasions greater mu-

[10] Harriet Martineau, "Preface," *The Positive Philosophy of Auguste Comte* (3 vols.; London: George Bell and Sons, 1896), I, xxx.

tual understanding—and perhaps even some consensus—might be reached on the conflict between religion and science. Although by 1880 it was clear that the differences between theism and rationalism would not yield to such palliatives, and the Society was disbanded, those eleven years of discussion had yielded a number of memorable essays which contributed significantly to the singular distinction of Victorian periodical literature. Many of the essays appeared in the *Contemporary Review*, which was edited by James Knowles, one of the founders of the Society. By March, 1877, however, Knowles had initiated his own monthly, the *Nineteenth Century*, and the deliberations of the Society began appearing in that journal. In discussions like those on "The Influence upon Morality of a Decline in Religious Belief" and "The Soul and Future Life" Mallock had a rich quarry of writing illustrative of modern thought.

These essays, together with the ensuing

commentaries, all appearing within a year of the publication of *The New Paul and Virginia,* provided Mallock with nearly half of the passages he cited in his notes as exhibits of positivist thought. A similar desire for contemporaneity inspired Mallock's choice of other passages for satiric treatment. Even the title seems to have been selected to capitalize on the current popularity of Bernardin de Saint-Pierre's *Paul et Virginie* and of an opera by Victor Massé based on that tale. Yet the title is somewhat misleading: Mallock's satire recalls Saint-Pierre's sentimental romance in little more than the names of the title characters and the motif of isolation on a tropical island. And if the immediate popularity of *The New Paul and Virginia* benefited from its topicality, Mallock, by addressing himself so specifically to the polemical wars of the century, lost the opportunity to write a more universal study of the moral implications of rationalist ethics.

Jerome H. Buckley has usefully suggested

the category of "burlesque-romance" for discussion of *The New Paul and Virginia*.[11] The
basic situation of the novel would seem to
be rich in romantic possibilities: a fashion-
able lady, traveling to join the colonial
bishop she had recently wed, and a renowned
philosopher, returning to his wife after a
lengthy absence, miraculously escape their
sinking ocean-steamer and float away in a
conveniently well-provisioned lifeboat until
they reach a nearby island, there to attempt
to fashion a utopian existence according to
the principles of modern thought. Yet the
apparently romantic is never far removed
from the burlesque. The philosopher, we
learn, had to escape his evangelical wife
because of her incessant carping over his disbelief in hell; the bishop's diocese is "the
Chasuble Islands"; and the island on which
the pair are stranded is replete with a fully

[11] *The Victorian Temper: A Study in Literary Cul-
ture* (Cambridge: Harvard University Press, 1951), p.
200.

furnished cottage, a bread tree which pro-
vides French rolls, and pigs which volunteer
to be eaten.

The absurdity of the setting affords an appropriate background for Mallock's demonstration of the absurdity of their enterprise.
With his frequent appeal to the precepts of
his positivist masters, Professor Paul Darnley
proves himself worthy of his fame as "a complete embodiment of enlightened modern
thought"; yet the life he fashions on the
island for himself and Virginia raises serious
questions as to the adequacy of the philosophy
he espouses. Paul and his pupil are continually torn between their professed devotion
to the abstraction of Humanity and their
subjection to the more concrete humanity of
their vanity, selfishness, and passion. Virginia's efforts to substitute Paul's rationalism for
her own Christianity are fumbling, at best.
And when, in her search for truth, she prac-
tices Paul's precepts, it is to her teacher's profound embarrassment. Paul, on the other

hand, is little more at ease in his positivist paradise; when confronted by genuine human emotion—most notably his love for Virginia—he is helpless.

The humorous results of Paul's attempt to mold human conduct according to a handful of positivist principles point to the inadequacy of those principles, at least in the simplistic form in which he presents them; human character is recalcitrant. As a foundation for happiness, altruism ("the sublime outcome of enlightened modern thought") proves a poor substitute for Christian principles. If, as Paul suggests, happiness in this world, and not salvation in the next, is the test of life's being worth living, it is clear that life, conducted according to his principles, is not. Paul and Virginia fail to achieve earthly happiness while they deny the possibility of any happiness elsewhere. Whatever the shortcomings of supernatural faith as a basis for morality, *The New Paul and Virginia* seeks to demonstrate that purely natural reason offers a hardly preferable alternative.

Much of the humor—and the satiric comment—of the book arises from the constant discrepancy between the sententiously optimistic rhetoric of Paul's theory and the dismal failure of his practice. Yet the reader misses the full power of Mallock's treatment of the morality of modern positivism if he sees merely the ludicrous character of life on the island. Beneath the amusing picture of existence there lies a grim suggestion of the degradation of life lived according to purely rational principles. While expounding "the Gospel of the kingdom of man," Paul is totally insensitive to the drowning of his fellow passengers; the death of a woman who appears briefly on the island is welcomed as contributing to "the greatest happiness of the greatest number"; another survivor of the shipwreck, a former curate lately converted to modern thought, turns to drink and in a stupor falls to his death; and Paul's final act before the shattering of his dream of creating

a positivist utopia is to hoot at the moon like
an owl. Mallock's point is clear to us: man,
living according to the principles of modern
thought, is reduced to the condition of an
animal.

Contemporaneous reviewers of the novel,
however, were apparently unmoved by either
Mallock's humor or his deeper philosophical
meaning. Though the book was frequently
reprinted during the nineteenth century both
in England and the United States, the reviewers were unenthusiastic. Remarking that "of
genuine humor there is not a trace" in the
book, the *Athenaeum* charged that Mallock
had not "even the *littérateur's* knowledge of
physics or metaphysics . . . . For such a writer
to throw ridicule upon some of the most
illustrious *savants* of the age is much as
though he should write a satire upon the
Indo-European theory of languages without
a knowledge of Sanscrit." The *Nation* (New
York) similarly questioned Mallock's understanding of positivist philosophy. "His satire

has no sting of truth, because he himself has no perception of the real significance of the doctrine he satirizes," the reviewer said. "Beneath the cleverness lies the hard Philistine rock, blind, impervious, barren." To those infatuated with the material and ethical "progress" of the nineteenth century, the book seemed reactionary and even impious, and Mallock himself a Philistine. *Scribner's Monthly* went so far as to argue that the thinkers he satirized "gained in luster not only in spite of but because of his attacks. They were the truly spiritual ones, the strivers, the representatives of Prometheus, while Mr. Mallock was the earth-spirit trying in vain to belittle their characters."[12] Several reviewers thought the novel not only unfair but also tasteless. The *Atlantic Monthly* found Mallock wanting in "the one indispensable requisite for a satirist," self-command: "Mr.

[12] *Athenaeum*, 20 July 1878, p. 69; *Nation*, 29 August 1878, pp. 133, 134; *Scribner's Monthly* 18 (1879), 789.

Mallock is so beside himself with anger that he falls into unpardonable coarseness . . . . In the more frantic transports . . . he is hardly quotable." For the *Catholic World,* the book was "too broad and farcical to please a fastidious taste." And the *British Quarterly Review* thought the book lacking "the reserve and delicacy that lie near to the finest reverence." Yet the magazine apparently confirmed the popular estimate of many readers when it concluded: "All we can do is to advise any of that class who have not yet read the 'New Paul and Virginia' to procure and to read it, for it is distinctly laughable and clever."[13]

Now, nearly a century after its initial publication, *The New Paul and Virginia* is once again available. It is no more likely today than in the nineteenth century to be judged a classic of English satire. But, freed from the "fastidious taste" of the Victorians, readers

[13] *Atlantic Monthly* 46 (1880), 767; *Catholic World* 29 (1879), 721; *British Quarterly Review* 68 (1878), 279.

can perhaps more fully enjoy the novel for its splendid entertainment. To the student of intellectual history, moreover, it will doubtless have a special interest. *The New Paul and Virginia* was written at a time when many were either enthusiastically committing themselves to the prospects of science, or wallowing in despair over the spiritual dislocations occasioned by Victorian rationalism, or retreating from the multitudinous pressures of nineteenth-century life into aestheticism. Mallock's novel bears witness to still another reaction, less popularly associated with the Victorians—the resort to humor, and satire in particular, as both a polemic and therapeutic tool.

A Note on the Text

The text of this edition of *The New Paul and Virginia* is reproduced from one of the several impressions printed from the plates of the first edition following its initial publication by Chatto and Windus in 1878. Collation of the present text with an earlier impression of the edition reveals no substantive variants between the two impressions. Some differences in accidentals—mutilated letters and punctuation marks, no doubt resulting from press damage—have been silently emended.

Mallock's "Notes" to the book have been retained. They are followed by the editor's supplementary notes, keyed to the page number of the text.

JOHN D. MARGOLIS

Northwestern University

STUDIES OF MALLOCK'S FICTION

A Selected Bibliography

Adams, Amy Belle. *The Novels of William Hurrell Mallock*. University of Maine Studies, 2d ser., no. 30. Orono, Me.: University Press, 1934.

Huneker, James. "On Rereading Mallock," in *Unicorns*, pp. 151–160. New York: Charles Scribner's Sons, 1917.

Lucas, John. "Tilting at the Moderns: W. H. Mallock's Criticisms of the Positivist Spirit." *Renaissance and Modern Studies* 10 (1966), 88–143.

Mallock, W. H. *The New Republic*. Edited by J. Max Patrick. Gainesville: University of Florida Press, 1950.

Margolis, John D. "W. H. Mallock's *The New Republic*: A Study in Late Victorian Satire." *English Literature in Transition* 10 (1967), 10–25.

Nickerson, Charles C. "A Bibliography of the Novels of W. H. Mallock." *English Literature in Transition* 6 (1963), 190–199.

Saintsbury, George. "Le Temps Jadis," in *A Second Scrap Book*, pp. 172–182. London: Macmillan and Co., Ltd., 1923.

Woodring, Carl R. "W. H. Mallock: A Neglected Wit." *More Books* 22 (1947), 243–256.

Yarker, P. M. "Voltaire among the Positivists: A Study of W. H. Mallock's *The New Paul and Virginia*." *Essays and Studies* n.s. 8 (1955), 21–39.

Yarker, P. M. "W. H. Mallock's Other Novels." *Nineteenth Century Fiction* 14 (1959), 189–205.

'Those who can read the signs of the times read in them that the kingdom of man is at hand '— Professor CLIFFORD

Thou art smitten, O God, thou art smitten ; thy curse is
    upon thee, O Lord !
And the love song of earth as thou diest, resounds through
    the wind of its wings,
Glory to man in the highest, for man is the master of
    things

Songs before Sunrise

THE

NEW PAUL AND VIRGINIA.

CHAPTER I.

THE magnificent ocean-steamer the *Australasian* was bound for England, on her homeward voyage from Melbourne, carrying Her Majesty's mails and ninety-eight first-class passengers. Never did vessel start under happier auspices. The skies were cloudless; the sea was smooth as glass. There was not a sound of sickness to

be heard anywhere; and when dinner-
time came there was not a single ab-
sentee nor an appetite wanting

But the passengers soon discovered
they were lucky in more than weather.
Dinner was hardly half over before two
of the company had begun to attract
general attention; and every one all
round the table was wondering, in whis-
pers, who they could possibly be.

One of the objects of this delightful
curiosity was a large-boned, middle-aged
man, with gleaming spectacles, and lank,
untidy hair; whose coat fitted him so ill,
and who held his head so high, that
one saw at a glance he was some great
celebrity. The other was a beautiful lady

of about thirty years of age, the like of whom nobody present had ever seen before. She had the fairest hair and the darkest eyebrows, the largest eyes and the smallest waist conceivable ; art and nature had been plainly struggling as to which should do the most for her ; whilst her bearing was so haughty and distinguished, her glance so tender, and her dress so expensive and so fascinating, that she seemed at the same time to defy and to court attention.

Evening fell on the ship with a soft warm witchery. The air grew purple, and the waves began to glitter in the moonlight. The passengers gathered in knots upon the deck, and the distinguished strangers were still the subject of conjecture. At last the secret was discovered by the wife of an old colonial judge ; and the news spread like wildfire. In a few minutes all knew that there were on board the *Australasian* no less personages than Professor Paul Darnley and the superb Virginia St. John.

CHAPTER II.

MISS ST. JOHN had, for at least six years, been the most renowned woman in Europe. In Paris and St. Petersburg, no less than in London, her name was equally familiar both to princes and to pot-boys ; indeed, the gaze of all the world was fixed on her. Yet, in spite of this exposed situation, scandal had proved powerless to wrong her ; she defied detraction. Her enemies could but echo her friends' praise

of her beauty; her friends could but con-
firm her enemies' description of her character. Though of birth that might almost
be called humble, she had been connected
with the heads of many distinguished
families; and so general was the affection
she inspired, and so winning the ways
in which she contrived to retain it, that
she found herself, at the age of thirty,
mistress of nothing except a large fortune. She was now converted with sur-
prising rapidity by a Ritualistic priest, and
she became in a few months a model
of piety and devotion. She made lace
trimmings for the curate's vestments;
she bowed at church as often and pro-
foundly as possible; she enjoyed nothing

so much as going to confession; she learnt to despise the world. Indeed, such utter dross did her riches now seem to her, that, despite all the arguments of her ghostly counsellor, she remained convinced that they were far too worthless to offer to the Church, and she saw nothing for it but to still keep them for herself. The mingled humility and discretion of this resolve so won the heart of a gifted colonial bishop, then on a visit to England, that, having first assured himself that Miss St. John was sincere in making it, he besought her to share with him his humble mitre, and make him the happiest prelate in the whole Catholic Church. Miss St. John consented. The nuptials were celebrated with the most elaborate ritual, and after a short honeymoon the bishop departed for his South Pacific diocese of the Chasuble Islands, to prepare a home for his bride, who was to follow him by the next steamer.

Professor Paul Darnley, in his own walk of life, was even more famous than Virginia had been in hers. He had written three volumes on the origin of life, which he had spent seven years in looking for in infusions of hay and cheese; he had written five volumes on the entozoa of the pig, and two volumes of lectures, as a corollary to these, on the sublimity of human heroism and the whole duty of man. He was renowned all over Europe and America as a complete embodiment of enlightened modern thought. He criticised everything; he took nothing on trust, except the unspeakable sublimity of the human race and its august terrestrial destinies. And, in his double capacity of a seer and a *savant*, he had destroyed all that the world had believed in the past, and revealed to it all that it is going to feel in the future. His mind indeed was like a sea, into which the other great minds of the age discharged themselves, and in which all the slight discrepancies of the philosophy of the present century mingled together and formed one harmonious whole. Nor was he less successful in his own private life. He

married, at the age of forty, an excellent
evangelical lady, ten years his senior, who
wore a green gown, grey corkscrew curls,
and who had a fortune of two hundred
thousand pounds. Deeply pledged though
she was to the most vapid figments of
Christianity, Mrs. Darnley was yet proud
beyond measure of her husband's world-
wide fame, for she did but imperfectly
understand the grounds of it. Indeed, the
only thing that marred her happiness was
the single tenet of his that she had really
mastered. This, unluckily, was that he disbelieved in hell. And so, as Mrs. Darnley conceived that that place was designed
mainly to hold those who doubted its
existence, she daily talked her utmost

and left no text unturned to convince her darling of his very dangerous error. These assiduous arguments soon began to tell. The Professor grew moody and brooding, and he at last suggested to his medical man that a voyage round the world, unaccompanied by his wife, was the prescription most needed by his failing patience. Mrs. Darnley at length consented with a fairly good grace. She made her husband pledge himself that he would not be absent for above a twelvemonth, or else, she said, she should immediately come after him. She bade him the tenderest of adieus, and promised to pray till his return for his recovery of a faith in hell.

The Professor, who had but exceeded his time by six months, was now on board the *Australasian*, homeward bound to his wife.   Virginia was outward bound to her husband.

CHAPTER III.

THE sensation created by the presence of these two celebrities was profound beyond description; and the passengers were never weary of watching the gleaming spectacles and the square-toed boots of the one, and the liquid eyes and the ravishing toilettes of the other. Virginia's acquaintance was made almost instantly by three pale-faced curates, and so well did their friendship prosper, that they soon sang at nightfall with her a beautiful vesper hymn. Nor did the matter end here, for the strains sounded so lovely, and Virginia looked so devotional, that most of the passengers the night after joined in a repetition of this touching evening office.

The Professor, as was natural, held quite aloof, and pondered over a new species of bug, which he had found very plentiful in his berth. But it soon occurred to him that he often heard the name of God being uttered otherwise than in swearing. He listened more attentively to the sounds which he had at first set down as negro-melodies, and he soon became convinced that they were something whose very existence he despised himself for re-membering — namely, Christian hymns. He then thought of the three curates, whose existence he despised himself for remembering also. And the conviction rapidly dawned on him that, though the passengers seemed fully alive to his fame as a man of science, they could yet know very little of all that science had done for them ; and of the death-blow it had given to the foul superstitions of the past. He therefore resolved that next day he would preach them a lay-sermon.

At the appointed time the passengers gathered eagerly round him—all but Virginia, who retired to her cabin when she saw that the preacher wore no surplice, as she thought it would be a mortal sin to listen to a sermon without one.

The Professor began amidst a profound silence. He first proclaimed to his hearers the great primary axiom on which all modern thought bases itself. He told them that there was but one order of things—it was so much neater than two ; and if we would be certain of anything, we must never doubt this. Thus, since countless things exist that the senses *can* take account of, it is evident that nothing exists that the senses can *not* take account of. The senses can take no account of God ; therefore God does not exist. Men of science can only see theology in a ridiculous light, therefore theology has no side that is not ridiculous. He then told them a few of the names that enlightened thinkers had applied to the Christian deity—how Professor Tyndall had called him an 'atom-manufacturer,' and Professor Huxley a 'pedantic drill-sergeant.' The passengers at once saw how demonstrably at variance with fact was all religion, and they laughed with a sense of humour that was quite new to them. The Professor's tones then became more solemn, and, having extinguished error, he at once went on to unveil the brilliant light of truth. He showed them how, viewed by modern

science, all existence is a chain, with a
gas at one end and no one knows what
at the other; and how Humanity is a
link somewhere; but—holy and awful
thought!—we can none of us tell where.
'However,' he proceeded, 'of one thing
we can be quite certain: all that is, is
matter; the laws of matter are eternal, and we cannot act or think without conforming to them; and if,' he said,
'we would be solemn and high, and
happy, and heroic, and saintly, we have
but to strive and struggle to do what
we cannot for an instant avoid doing.
Yes,' he exclaimed, 'as the sublime
Tyndall tells us, let us struggle to at-
tain to a deeper knowledge of matter,

and a more faithful conformity to its laws !'

The Professor would have proceeded, but the weather had been rapidly growing rough, and he here became violently sea-sick.

'Let us,' he exclaimed hurriedly, 'conform to the laws of matter and go below.'

Nor was the advice premature. A storm arose, exceptional in its suddenness and its fury. It raged for two days without ceasing. The *Australasian* sprang a leak ; her steering gear was disabled ; and it was feared she would go ashore on an island that was seen dimly through the fog to the leeward. The

boats were got in readiness. A quantity
of provisions and of the passengers'
baggage was already stowed in the cutter; when the clouds parted, the sun
came out again, and the storm subsided
almost as quickly as it rose.

CHAPTER IV.

NO sooner were the ship's damages in a fair way to be repaired than the Professor resumed his sermon. He climbed into the cutter, which was still full of the passengers' baggage, and sat down on the largest of Virginia's boxes. This so alarmed Virginia that she incontinently followed the Professor into the cutter, to keep an eye on her property; but she did not forget to stop her ears with her fingers, that she might not be guilty of listening to an unsurpliced minister.

The Professor took up the thread of his discourse just where he had broken it off. Every circumstance favoured him. The calm sea was sparkling under the gentlest breeze; all Nature seemed suffused with gladness; and at two miles' distance was an enchanting island, green with every kind of foliage, and glowing with the hues of a thousand flowers. The Professor, having reminded his hearers of what nonsense they now thought all the Christian teachings, went on to show them the blessed results of this. Since the God that we once called all-holy is a fable, that Humanity is all-holy must be a fact. Since we shall never be sublime, and solemn, and unspeakably happy hereafter, it is evident that we can be sublime, and solemn, and unspeakably happy here. 'This,' said the Professor, 'is the new Gospel. It is founded on exact thought. It is the Gospel of the kingdom of man; and had I only here a microscope and a few chemicals, I could demonstrate its eternal truth to you. There is no heaven to seek for; there is no hell to shun. We have nothing to strive and live for except to be unspeakably happy.'

This eloquence was received with enthusiasm. The captain in particular,

who had a wife in every port he
touched at, was overjoyed at hearing
that there was no hell; and he sent
for all the crew, that they might learn
the good news likewise. But soon the
general gladness was marred by a sound
of weeping. Three-fourths of the passengers, having had time to reflect a little,
began exclaiming that as a matter of fact
they were really completely miserable,
and that for various reasons they could
never be anything else. 'My friends,'
said the Professor, quite undaunted,
'that is doubtless completely true. You
are not happy now; you probably never
will be. But that, I can assure you, is of
very little moment. Only conform faith-

fully to the laws of matter, and your children's children will be happy in the course of a few centuries; and you will like that far, far better than being happy yourselves. Only consider the matter in ˙this light, and you yourselves will in an instant become happy also; and whatever you say, and whatever you do, think only of the effect it will have five hundred years afterwards.'

At these solemn words, the anxious faces grew calm. An awful sense of the responsibility of each one of us, and the infinite consequences of every human act, was filling the hearts of all; when by a faithful conformity to the laws of matter, the boiler blew up,

and the *Australasian* went down. In
an instant the air was rent with yells
and cries; and all the Humanity that
was on board the vessel was busy, as
the Professor expressed it, uniting itself
with the infinite azure of the past.
Paul and Virginia, however, floated
quietly away in the cutter, together
with the baggage and provisions.

Virginia was made almost senseless
by the suddenness of the catastrophe; and
on seeing five sailors sink within three
yards of her, she fainted dead away.
The Professor begged her not to take
it so much to heart, as these were the
very men who had got the cutter in
readiness; 'and they are, therefore,' he

said, 'still really alive in the fact of our happy escape.' Virginia, however, being quite insensible, the Professor turned to the last human being still to be seen above the waters, and shouted to him not to be afraid of death, as there was certainly no hell, and that his life, no matter how degraded and miserable, had been a glorious mystery, full of infinite significance. The next moment the struggler was snapped up by a shark. Our friends, meanwhile, borne by a current, had been drifting rapidly towards the island. And the Professor, spreading to the breeze Virginia's beautiful lace parasol, soon brought the cutter to the shore on a beach of the softest sand.

CHAPTER V.

THE scene that met Paul's eyes was one of extreme loveliness. He found himself in a little fairy bay, full of translucent waters, and fringed with silvery sands. On either side it was protected by fantastic rocks, and in the middle it opened inland to an enchanting valley, where tall tropical trees made a grateful shade, and where the ground was carpeted with the softest moss and turf.

Paul's first care was for his fair companion. He spread a costly cashmere shawl on the beach, and placed her, still fainting, on this. In a few moments she opened her eyes; but was on the point of fainting again as the horrors of the last half-hour came back to her, when she caught sight in the cutter of the largest of her own boxes, and she began to recover herself. Paul begged her to remain quiet whilst he went to reconnoitre.

He had hardly proceeded twenty yards into the valley, when to his infinite astonishment he came on a charming cottage, built under the shadow of a bread-tree, with a broad verandah, plate-glass windows, and red window-blinds. His first thought was that this could be no desert island at all, but some happy European settlement. But, on approaching the cottage, it proved to be quite untenanted, and from the cob-webs woven across the doorway it seemed to have been long abandoned. Inside there was abundance of luxurious fur-niture; the floors were covered with gorgeous Indian carpets; and there was a pantry well stocked with plate and glass and table-linen. The Professor could not tell what to make of it, till, examining the structure more closely, he found it composed mainly of a ship's timbers. This seemed to tell its own tale, and he at once concluded that he and Virginia were not the first castaways who had been forced to make the island for some time their dwelling-place.

Overjoyed at this discovery, he hastened back to Virginia. She was by this time apparently quite recovered, and was kneeling on the cashmere shawl, with a rosary in her hands designed especially for the use of Anglo-Catholics, alternately lifting up her eyes in gratitude to heaven, and casting them down in anguish at her torn and crumpled dress. The poor Professor was horrified at the sight of a human being

in this degrading attitude of superstition.
But as Virginia quitted it with alacrity
as soon as ever he told his news to her,
he hoped he might soon convert her into
a sublime and holy Utilitarian.

The first thing she besought him to
do was to carry her biggest box to
this charming cottage, that she might
change her clothes, and appear in
something fit to be seen in. The
Professor most obligingly at once did
as she asked him ; and whilst she was
busy at her toilette, he got from the
cutter what provisions he could, and
proceeded to lay the table. When all
was ready, he rang a gong which he
found suspended in the lobby ; Virginia

appeared shortly in a beautiful pink
dressing-gown, embroidered with silver
flowers ; and just before sunset the two
sat down to a really excellent meal.
The bread tree at the door of the cottage contributed some beautiful French
rolls ; close at hand also they discovered
a butter-tree ; and the Professor had
produced from the cutter a variety of
salt and potted meats, *pâté de foie gras,*
cakes, preserved fruits, and some bottles
of fine champagne. This last helped
much to raise their spirits. Virginia
found it very dry, and exactly suited to
her palate. She had but drunk five
glasses of it, when her natural smile
returned to her, though she was much

disappointed because Paul took no no-
tice of her dressing-gown, and when she
had drunk three glasses more she quietly
went to sleep on the sofa.

The moon had by this time risen in
dazzling splendour, and the Professor
went out and lighted a cigar. All
during dinner there had been a feeling
of dull despair in his heart, which even
the champagne did not dissipate. But
now, as he surveyed in the moonlight
the wondrous Paradise in which his
strange fate had cast him, his mood
changed. The air was full of the scents
of a thousand night-smelling flowers;
the sea murmured on the beach in soft,
voluptuous cadences. The Professor's

cigar was excellent. He now saw his situation in a truer light. Here was a bountiful island, where earth unbidden brought forth all her choicest fruits, and most of the luxuries of civilisation had already been wafted thither. Existence here seemed to be purified from all its evils. Was not this the very condition of things which all the sublimest and exactest thinkers of modern times had been dreaming and lecturing and writing books about for a good half-century? Here was a place where Humanity could do justice to itself, and realise those glorious destinies which all exact thinkers take for granted must be in store for it. True, from the mass of Humanity he was completely cut away; but Virginia was his companion. Holiness, and solemnity, and unspeakably significant happiness did not, he argued, depend on the multiplication table. He and Virginia represented Humanity as well as a million couples. They were a complete humanity in themselves, and humanity in a perfectible shape; and the very next day they would make preparations for fulfilling their holy destiny, and being as solemnly and unspeakably happy as it was their stern duty to be.

The Professor turned his eyes upwards to the starry heavens, and a sense came over him of the eternity and the immensity of Nature, and the demonstrable absence of any intelligence that guided it. These reflections naturally brought home to him with more vividness the stupendous and boundless importance of Man. His bosom swelled violently, and he cried aloud, his eyes still fixed on the firmament, 'Oh, important All! oh, important Me!'

When he came back to the cottage he found Virginia just getting off the sofa, and preparing to go to bed. She was too sleepy even to say good-night to him, and with evident want of temper was tugging at the buttons of her dressing-gown. 'Ah!' she murmured as she left the room, 'if God, in His infinite mercy, had only spared my maid!'

Virginia's evident discontent gave profound pain to Paul. 'How solemn,' he exclaimed, 'for half Humanity to be discontented!' But he was still more disturbed at the appeal to a chimerical manufacturer of atoms; and he groaned in tones of yet more sonorous sorrow, 'How solemn for half Humanity to be sunk lower than the beasts by superstition!'

However, he hoped that these stupendous evils might, under the present favourable conditions, vanish in the course of a few days' progress; and he went to bed, full of august auguries.

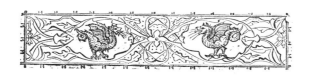

CHAPTER VI.

NEXT morning he was up be-
times; and the prospects of
Humanity looked more glo-
rious than ever. He gathered some of
the finest pats from the butter-tree, and
some fresh French rolls from the bread-
tree. He discovered a cow close at hand,
that allowed him at once to milk it;
and a little roast pig ran up to him out
of the underwood, and fawning on him
with its trotters, said, 'Come, eat me.

The Professor vivisected it before Virginia's door, that its automatic noise, which the vulgar call cries of pain, might awaken her; and he then set it in a hot dish on the table.

'It has come! it has come!' he shouted, rapturously, as Virginia entered the room, this time in a blue silk dressing-gown, embroidered with flowers of gold.

'What has come?' said Virginia, pettishly, for she was suffering from a terrible headache, and the Professor's loud voice annoyed her. 'You don't mean to say that we are rescued, are we?'

'Yes,' answered Paul, solemnly; 'we are rescued. We are rescued from all the pains and imperfections of a world that has not learnt how to conform to the laws of matter, and is but imperfectly acquainted with the science of sociology. It is therefore inevitable that, the evils of existence being thus removed, we shall both be solemnly, stupendously, and unspeakably happy.'

' Nonsense!' said Virginia, snappishly, who thought the Professor was joking.

' It is not nonsense,' said the Professor. ' It is deducible from the teachings of John Stuart Mill, of Auguste Comte, of Mr. Frederic Harrison, and of all the exact thinkers who have cast off superstition, and who adore Humanity.'

Virginia meanwhile ate *pâté de foie gras*, of which she was passionately fond;

and, growing a little less sullen, she at
last admitted that they were lucky in
having at least the necessaries of life left
to them.   'But as for happiness—there
is nothing to do here, there is no church
to go to, and you don't seem to care a
bit for my dressing-gown.   What have
we got to make us happy ?'

'Humanity,' replied the Professor
eagerly,—'Humanity, that divine entity,
which is necessarily capable of everything
that is fine and invaluable, and is the
object of indescribable emotion to all
exact thinkers.   And what is Humanity?'
he went on more earnestly; 'you and I
are Humanity—you and I are that august
existence.   You already are all the world

to me ; and I very soon shall be all the world to you. Adored being, it will be my mission and my glory to compel you to live for me. And then, as modern philosophy can demonstrate, we shall both of us be significantly and unspeakably happy.'

For a few moments Virginia merely stared at Paul. Suddenly she turned quite pale, her lips quivered, and exclaiming, 'How dare you !—and I, too, the wife of a bishop !' she left the room in hysterics.

The Professor could make nothing of this. Though he had dissected many dead women, he knew very little of the hearts of live ones. A sense of shyness overpowered him, and he felt embarrassed, he could not tell why, at being thus left alone with Virginia. He lit a cigar and went out. Here was a to-do indeed, he thought. How would progress be possible if one half of Humanity misunderstood the other?

He was thus musing, when suddenly a voice startled him; and in another moment a man came rushing up to him, with every demonstration of joy.

'Oh, my dear master! oh, emancipator of the human intellect! and is it indeed you? Thank God !——I beg pardon for my unspeakable blasphemy — I mean, thank circumstances over which I have no control.'

It was one of the three curates, whom Paul had supposed drowned, but who now related how he had managed to swim ashore, despite the extreme length of his black clerical coat. 'These rags of superstition,' he said, 'did their best to drown me. But I survive in spite of them, to covet truth and to reject error. Thanks to your glorious teaching,' he went on, looking reverentially into the Professor's face, 'the very notion of an Almighty Father makes me laugh consumedly, it is so absurd and so immoral. Science, through your instrumentality, has opened my eyes. I am now an exact thinker.'

'Do you believe,' said Paul, 'in solemn,

significant, and unspeakably happy Humanity ?'

'I do,' said the curate, fervently. 'Whenever I think of Humanity, I groan and moan to myself out of sheer solemnity.'

'Then two thirds of Humanity,' said the Professor, 'are thoroughly enlightened. Progress will now go on smoothly.'

At this moment Virginia came out, having rapidly recovered composure at the sound of a new man's voice.

'You here—you, too !' exclaimed the curate. 'How solemn, how significant ! This is truly Providential——I mean this has truly happened through conformity to the laws of matter.'

'Well,' said Virginia, 'since we have a clergyman amongst us, we shall perhaps be able to get on.'

CHAPTER VII.

THINGS now took a better turn. The Professor ceased to feel shy; and proposed, when the curate had finished an enormous breakfast, that they should go down to the cutter, and bring up the things in it to the cottage. 'A few hours' steady progress,' he said, 'and the human race will command all the luxuries of civilisation— the glorious fruits of centuries of onward labour.

The three spent a very busy morning in examining and unpacking the luggage. The Professor found his favourite collection of modern philosophers; Virginia found a large box of knick-knacks, with which to adorn the cottage; and there was, too, an immense store of wine and of choice provisions.

'It is rather sad,' sighed Virginia, as she dived into a box of French chocolate-creams, 'to think that all the poor people are drowned that these things belonged to.'

'They are not dead,' said the Professor: 'they still live on this holy and stupendous earth. They live in the use we are making of all they had got

together. The owner of those chocolate-creams is immortal because you
are eating them.'

Virginia licked her lips and said,
'Nonsense!'

'It is not nonsense,' said the Professor. 'It is the religion of Humanity.'

All day they were busy, and the
time passed pleasantly enough. Wines,
provisions, books, and china ornaments
were carried up to the cottage and
bestowed in proper places. Virginia
filled the glasses in the drawing-room
with gorgeous leaves and flowers and
declared by the evening, as she looked
round her, that she could almost fancy
herself in St. John's Wood.

'See,' said the Professor, 'how rapid is the progress of material civilisation! Humanity is now entering on the fruits of ages. Before long it will be in a position to be unspeakably happy.'

Virginia retired to bed early. The Professor took the curate out with him to look at the stars ; and promised to lend him some writings of the modern philosophers, which would make him more perfect in the new view of things. They said good-night, murmuring to-gether that there was certainly no God, that Humanity was very important, and that everything was very solemn.

CHAPTER VIII.

NEXT morning the curate began studying a number of essays that the Professor lent him, all written by exact thinkers, who disbelieved in God, and thought Humanity adorable, and most important. Virginia lay on the sofa, and sighed over one of Miss Broughton's novels; and it occurred to the Professor that the island was just the place where, if anywhere, the missing link might be found.

'Ah!' he exclaimed; 'all is still progress. Material progress came to an
end yesterday. Mental progress has
begun to-day. One third of Humanity
is cultivating sentiment; another third
is learning to covet truth. I, the remaining and most enlightened third, will
go and seek it. Glorious, solemn Humanity! I will go and look about for
its arboreal ancestor.'

Every step the Professor took he
found the island more beautiful. But
he came back to luncheon, having been
unsuccessful in his search. Events had
marched quickly in his absence. Virginia was at the beginning of her third
volume; and the curate had skimmed

over so many essays, that he professed himself able to give a thorough account of the want of faith that was in him.

After luncheon the three sat together in easy chairs, in the verandah, sometimes talking, sometimes falling into a half-doze. They all agreed that they were wonderfully comfortable, and the Professor said—

'All Humanity is now at rest, and in utter peace. It is just taking breath, before it becomes unspeakably and significantly happy.'

He would have said more, but he was here startled by a piteous noise of crying, and the three found themselves confronted by an old woman dripping with sea-water, and with an expression on her face of the utmost misery. They soon recognised her as one of the passengers on the ship. She told them how she had been floated ashore on a spar, and how she had been sustained by a little roast pig, that kindly begged her to eat it, having first lain in her bosom to restore her to warmth. She was now looking for her son.

'And if I cannot find him,' said the old woman, 'I shall never smile again. He has half broken my heart,' she went on, 'by his wicked ways. But if I thought he was dead—dead in the midst of his sins—it would be broken altogether; for in that case he must certainly be in hell.'

'Old woman,' said the Professor, very slowly and solemnly, 'be comforted. I announce to you that your son is alive.'

'Oh, bless you, sir, for that word!' cried the old woman. 'But where is he? Have you seen him? Are you sure that he is living?'

'I am sure of it,' said the Professor, 'because enlightened thought shows me that he cannot be anything else. It is true that I saw him sink for a third time in the sea, and that he was then snapped up by a shark. But he is as much alive as ever in his posthumous activities. He has made you wretched after him; and that is his future life. Become an exact thinker, and you will see that this is so. Old woman,' added the Professor solemnly, 'old woman, listen to me—*You are your son in hell.*'

At this the old woman flew into a terrible rage.

'In hell, sir!' she exclaimed; 'me in hell!—a poor lone woman like me! How dare you!' And she sank back in a chair and fainted.

'Alas!' said the Professor, 'thus is misery again introduced into the world. A fourth part of Humanity is now miserable.'

The curate answered promptly that

if no restoratives were given her, she would probably die in a few minutes. 'And to let her die,' he said, 'is clearly our solemn duty. It will be for the greatest happiness of the greatest number.'

'No,' said the Professor; 'for our sense of pity would then be wounded, and the happiness of all of us would be marred by that.'

'Excuse me,' said the curate; 'but exact thought shows me that pity for others is but the imagining of their misfortune falling on ourselves. Now, we can none of us imagine ourselves exactly in the old woman's case; there-fore it is quite impossible that we can pity her.'

'But,' said the Professor, 'such an act would violate our ideas of justice.'

'You are wrong again,' said the curate, 'for exact thought shows me that the love of justice is nothing but the fear of suffering injustice. If we were to kill strong men, we might naturally fear that strong men would kill us. But whatever we do to fainting old women, we cannot expect that fainting old women will do anything to us in return.'

'Your reasoning cannot be sound,' said the Professor, 'for it would lead to the most horrible conclusions. I will solve the difficulty better. I will make the old woman happy, and therefore fit to live. Old woman,' he exclaimed, 'let

me beg you to consider this. You are
yourself by your own unhappiness ex-
piating your son's sins. Do but think of
that, and you will become unspeakably
happy.'

Meanwhile, however, the old woman
had died. When the Professor discovered
this he was somewhat shocked; but at
length with a sudden change of counte-
nance, 'We neither of us did it,' he exclaimed; 'her death is no act of ours.
It is part of the eternal not-ourselves
that makes for righteousness—righteousness, which is, as we all know, but
another name for happiness. Let us
adore the event with reverence.'

'Yes,' said the curate, 'we are well rid

of her. She was an immoral old woman, for happiness is the test of morality, and she was very unhappy.'

'On the contrary,' said the Professor, 'she was a moral old woman; for she has made us happy by dying so very opportunely. Let us speak well of the dead. Her death has been a holy and a blessed one. She has conformed to the laws of matter. Thus is unhappiness destined to fade out of the world. Quick! let us tie a bag of shot to all the sorrow and evil of Humanity, which, after all, is only a fourth part of it, and let us sink her in the bay close at hand, that she may catch lobsters for us.'

CHAPTER IX.

'AT last,' said the Professor, as they began dinner that evening, 'the fulness of time has come. All the evils of Humanity are removed, and progress has come to an end because it can go no further. We have nothing now to do but to be unspeakably and significantly happy.'

The champagne flowed freely. Our friends ate and drank of the best, their spirits rose, and Virginia admitted that this was really 'jolly.' The sense of the word pleased the Professor, but its sound seemed below the gravity of the occasion; so he begged her to say 'sublime' instead. 'We can make it mean,' he said, 'just the same, but we prefer it for the sake of its associations.'

It soon, however, occurred to him that eating and drinking were hardly delights sufficient to justify the highest state of human emotion, and he began to fear he had been feeling sublime prematurely; but in another moment he recollected he was an altruist, and that the secret of their happiness was not that any one of them was happy, but that they each knew the others were.

'Yes, my dear curate,' said the Professor, 'what I am enjoying is the champagne that you drink, and what you are
enjoying is the champagne that I drink.
This is altruism; this is benevolence;
this is the sublime outcome of enlightened
modern thought. The pleasures of the
table, in themselves, are low and beastly
ones; but if we each of us are only glad
because the others are enjoying them,
they become holy and glorious beyond
description.'

'They do,' cried the curate rapturously, 'indeed they do. I will drink
another bottle for your sake. It is sublime!' he said, as he tossed off three
glasses. 'It is significant!' he said as

he finished three more. 'Tell me, my dear, do I look significant?' he added, as he turned to Virginia, and suddenly tried to crown the general bliss by kissing her.

Virginia started back, looking fire and fury at him. The Professor was completely astounded by an occurrence so unnatural, and exclaimed in a voice of thunder, 'Morality, sir—remember morality! How dare you upset that which Professor Huxley tells us must be for ever strong enough to hold its own?'

But the last glass of champagne had put the curate beyond the reach of exact thought. He tumbled under the table, and the Professor carried him off to bed.

CHAPTER X.

THE Professor, like most serious thinkers, knew but little of that trifle commonly called 'the world.' He had never kissed any one except his wife; even that he did as seldom as possible; and the curate lying dead drunk was the first glimpse he had of what, *par excellence*, is described as 'life.' But though the scene just recounted was thus a terrible shock to him, in one way it gave him an unlooked-for comfort. He had felt that even yet things were not quite as sublime as they should be. He now saw the reason. 'Of course,' he said, 'existence cannot be perfect so long as one third of Humanity makes a beast of itself. A little more progress must be still necessary.'

He hastened to explain this next morning to Virginia, and begged her not to be alarmed at the curate's scandalous conduct. 'Immorality,' he said, 'is but a want of success in attaining our own happiness. It is evidently most immoral for the curate to be kissing you ; and therefore kissing you would not really conduce to his happiness. I will convince him of this solemn truth in a very

few moments. Then the essential dignity of human nature will become at
once apparent, and we shall all of us at
last begin to be unspeakably happy.'

The curate, however, altogether declined to be convinced. He maintained
stoutly that to kiss Virginia would be the
greatest pleasure that Humanity could
offer him. 'And if it is immoral as well
as pleasant,' he added, 'I should like it
all the better.'

At this the Professor gave a terrible
groan ; he dropped almost fainting into
a chair ; he hid his face in his hands ;
and murmured half-articulately, 'Then I
can't tell what to do !' In another instant, however, he recovered himself ; and

fixing a dreadful look on the curate, 'That last statement of yours,' he said, 'cannot be true; for if it were, it would upset all my theories. It is a fact that can be proved and verified, that if you kissed Virginia it would make you miserable.'

'Pardon me,' said the curate, rapidly moving towards her, 'your notion is a remnant of superstition; I will explode it by a practical experiment.'

The Professor caught hold of the curate's coat-tails, and forcibly pulled him back into his seat.

'If you dare attempt it,' he said, 'I will kick you soundly; and, shocking, immoral man! you will feel miserable enough then.'

The curate was a terrible coward, and very weak as well. 'You are a great hulking fellow,' he said, eyeing the Professor; 'and I am of a singularly delicate build. I must, therefore, conform to the laws of matter, and give in.' He said this in a very sulky voice; and, going out of the room, slammed the door after him.

A radiant expression suffused the face of the Professor. 'See,' he said to Virginia, 'the curate's conversion is already half accomplished. In a few hours more he will be rational, he will be moral, he will be solemnly and significantly happy.'

The Professor talked like this to Virginia the whole morning; but in spite of all his arguments, she declined to be comforted. ' It is all very well,' she said, ' whilst you are in the way. But as soon as your back is turned, I know he will be at me again.'

' Will you never,' said Paul, by this time a little irritated, ' will you never listen to exact thought ? The curate is now reflecting ; and a little reflection must inevitably convince him that he does not really care to kiss you, and that it would give him very little real pleasure to do so.'

' Stuff ! ' exclaimed Virginia, with a sudden vigour at which the Professor was thunderstruck. ' I can tell you,' she went on, ' that better men than he have borne kicks for my sake; and to kiss me is the only thing that that little man cares about.—What *shall* I do?' she exclaimed, bursting into tears.   'Here is one of you insulting me by trying to kiss me; and the other insulting me by saying that I am not worth being kissed!'

'Ah, me!' groaned the poor Professor in an agony, 'here is one third of Humanity plunged in sorrow; and another third has not yet freed itself from vice. When, when, I wonder, will the sublimity begin?'

CHAPTER XI.

AT dinner, however, things wore a more promising aspect. The curate had been so terrified by the Professor's threats, that he hardly dared to so much as look at Virginia; and to make up for it, he drank and drank champagne, till the strings of his tongue were loosed, and he was laughing and chattering at a rate that was quite extraordinary. Virginia, seeing herself thus neglected by the curate, began to fear that, as

Paul said, he really did not so much care to kiss her after all. She, therefore, put on all her most enticing ways ; she talked, flirted, and smiled her best, and made her most effective eyes, that the curate might see what a prize was for ever beyond his reach.

This state of affairs seemed full of glorious promise. Virginia's tears were dried, she had never looked so radiant and exquisite before. The curate had foregone every attempt to kiss Virginia, and yet apparently he was happiness itself ; and Paul took him aside, as soon as the meal was over, to congratulate him on the holy state to which exact thought had conducted him. ' You see,'

Paul said, 'what a natural growth the loftiest morality is. Virginia doesn't want to be kissed by you. I should be shocked at your doing so shocking a thing as kissing her. If you kissed her, you would make both of us miserable; and, as a necessary consequence, you would be in an agony likewise; in addition to which, I should inevitably kick you.'

'But,' said the curate, 'suppose I kissed Virginia on the sly,—I merely put this as an hypothesis, remember,—and that in a little while she liked it, what then? She and I would both be happy, and you ought to be happy too, because we were.'

'Idiot!' said the Professor. 'Virginia is another man's wife. Nobody really likes kissing another man's wife; nor do wives ever like kissing any one except their husbands. What they really like is what Professor Huxley calls "the undefined but bright ideal of the highest good," which, as he says, exact thought shows us is the true end of existence. But, pooh! what is the use of all this talking? You know which way your higher nature calls you; and, of course, unless men believe in God, they cannot help obeying their higher nature.'

'I,' said the curate, 'think the belief in God a degrading superstition; I think every one an imbecile who believes a miracle possible. And yet I do not care two straws about the highest good. What you call my lower nature is far the strongest: I mean to follow it to the best of my ability; and I prefer calling it my higher, for the sake of the associations.'

This plunged the Professor in deeper grief than ever. He knew not what to do. He paced up and down the verandah, or about the rooms, and moaned and groaned as if he had a violent toothache. Virginia and the curate asked what was amiss with him. 'I am agonising,' he said, 'for the sake of holy, solemn, unspeakably dignified Humanity.'

The curate, seeing the Professor thus

dejected, by degrees took heart again ;
and as Virginia still continued her fascinating behaviour to him, he resolved to
try and prove to her that, the test of
morality being happiness, the most moral
thing she could do would be to allow
him to kiss her.   No sooner had he
begun to propound these views, than the
Professor · gave over his groaning, seized
the curate by the collar, and dragged
him out of the room with a roughness
that nearly throttled him.

'I was but propounding a theory—
an opinion,' gasped the curate.   'Surely
thought is free.   You will not persecute
me for my opinions ? '

'It is not for your opinions,' said the

Professor, 'but for the horrible effect they might have. Opinions,' he roared, ' can only be tolerated which have no possible consequences. You may promulgate any of those as much as you like ; because to do that would be a self-regarding action.'

CHAPTER XII.

'WELL,' said the curate, 'if I may not kiss Virginia, I will drink brandy instead. That will make me happy enough; and then we shall all be radiant.'

He soon put his resolve into practice. He got a bottle of brandy, he sat himself down under a palm-tree, and told the Professor he was going to make an afternoon of it.

'Foolish man!' said the Professor; 'I was never drunk myself, it is true; but I know that to get drunk makes one's head ache horribly. To get drunk is, therefore, horribly immoral; and therefore I cannot permit it.'

'Excuse me,' said the curate; 'it is a self-regarding action. Nobody's head will ache but mine; so that is my own look-out. I have been expelled from school, from college, and from my first curacy for drinking. So I know well enough the balance of pains and pleasures.'

Here he pulled out his brandy bottle, and applied his lips to it.

'Oh, Humanity!' he exclaimed, 'how solemn this brandy tastes!'

Matters went on like this for several days. The curate was too much frightened to again approach Virginia. Virginia at last became convinced that he did not care about kissing her. Her vanity was wounded, and she became sullen; and this made the Professor sullen also. In fact, two thirds of Humanity were overcast with gloom. The only happy section of it was the curate, who alternately smoked and drank all day long.

'The nasty little beast!' said Virginia to the Professor; 'he is nearly always drunk. I am beginning quite to like you, Paul, by comparison with him. Let us turn him out, and not let him live in the cottage.'

'No,' said the Professor; 'for he is one third of Humanity. You do not properly appreciate the solidarity of mankind. His existence, however, I admit is a great difficulty.'

One day at dinner-time, shortly afterwards, Paul came in radiant.

'Oh holy, oh happy event!' he exclaimed; 'all will go right at last.'

Virginia inquired anxiously what had happened, and Paul informed her that the curate, who had got more drunk than usual that afternoon, had fallen over a cliff, and been dashed to pieces.

'What event,' he asked, 'could be more charming—more unspeakably holy? It bears about it every mark of sanctity. It is for the greatest happiness of the greatest number. Come,' he continued, 'let you and me together, purged of sin, and purged of sorrow as we are—let us begin our love-feast. Let us each seek the happiness of the other. Let us instantly be sublime and happy.'

CHAPTER XIII.

'THE supreme moment is come,' said Paul solemnly, as they sat down to dinner. 'Let us prepare ourselves for realising to the full the essential dignity of Humanity—that *grand être*, which has come, in the course of progress, to consist of you and me. Virginia, consider this. Every condition of happiness that modern thinkers have dreamed of is now fulfilled. We have but to seek each the happiness of the other, and we shall both be in a solemn, a significant, and unspeakable state of rapture.   See, here is an exquisite leg of mutton. I,' said Paul, who liked the fat best, 'will give up all the fat to you.'

'And I,' said Virginia, resignedly, 'will give up all the lean to you.'

A few mouthfuls made Virginia feel sick. ' I confess,' said she, ' I can't get on with this fat.'

' I confess,' the Professor answered, ' I don't exactly like this lean.'

' Then let us,' said Virginia, ' be like Jack Sprat and his wife.'

' No,' said the Professor, meditatively, ' that is quite inadmissible.   For in that case we should be egoistic hedonists.

However, for to-day it shall be as you say. I will think of something better to-morrow.'

Next day he and Virginia had a chicken apiece; only Virginia's was put before Paul, and Paul's before Virginia; and they each walked round the table to supply each other with the slightest necessaries.

'Ah!' cried Paul, 'this is altruism indeed. I think already I can feel the sublimity beginning.'

Virginia liked this rather better. But soon she committed the sin of taking for herself the liver of Paul's chicken. As soon as she had eaten the whole of it her conscience began to smite her. She

confessed her sin to Paul, and inquired,
with some anxiety, if he thought she
would go to hell for it. 'Metaphorically,'
said Paul, 'you have already done so.
You are punished by the loss of the
pleasure you would have had in giving
that liver to me, and also by your knowledge of my knowledge of your folly in
foregoing the pleasure.'

Virginia was much relieved by this
answer; she at once took several more
of the Professor's choicest bits, and was
happy in the thought that her sins were
expiated in the very act of their com-
mission, by the latent pain she felt per-
suaded they were attended by. Feeling
that this was sufficient, she took care

not to add Paul's disapproval to her punishment, so she never told him again.

For a short time this practice of altruism seemed to Virginia to have many advantages. But though the Professor was always exclaiming, 'How significant is human life by the very nature of its constitution!' she very soon found it a trifle dull. Luckily, however, she hit upon a new method of exercising morality, and, as the Professor fully admitted, of giving it a yet more solemn significance.

The Professor having by some accident lost his razors, his moustaches had begun to grow profusely, and Virginia had watched them with a deep but half-conscious admiration. At last, in a happy moment, she exclaimed, 'Oh, Paul, do let me wax the ends for you.' Paul at first giggled, blushed, and protested, but, as Virginia assured him it would make her happy, he consented. 'Then,' she said, 'you will know that I am happy, and that in return will make you happy also. Ah!' she exclaimed when the operation was over, 'do go and examine yourself in the glass. I declare you look exactly like Jack Barley—Barley-Sugar, as we used to call him—of the Blues.'

Virginia smiled; suddenly she blushed; the Professor blushed also. To cover the blushes she begged to be allowed to do his hair. 'It will make me so

much happier, Paul,' she said. The
Professor again assented, that he might
make Virginia happy, and that she might
be happy in knowing that he was
happy in promoting her happiness. At
last the Professor, shy and awkward as
he was, was emboldened to offer to do
Virginia's hair in return. She allowed
him to arrange her fringe, and, as she
found he did no great harm to it, she let
him repeat the operation as often as he
liked.

A week thus passed, full, as the Professor said, of infinite solemnity. 'I
admit, Paul,' sighed Virginia, 'that this
altruism, as you call it, is very touching.
I like it very much. But,' she added,

sinking her voice to a whisper, 'are you quite sure, Paul, that it is perfectly moral ?'

'Moral !' echoed the Professor, 'moral ! Why, exact thought shows us that it is the very essence of all morality !'

CHAPTER XIV.

MATTERS now went on charmingly. All existence seemed to take a richer colouring, and there was something, Paul said, which, in Professor Tyndall's words, 'gave fulness and tone to it, but which he could neither analyse nor comprehend.' But at last a change came. One morning, whilst Virginia was arranging Paul's moustaches, she was frightened almost into a fit by a sudden apparition at the window. It was a hideous hairy figure, perfectly naked but for a band of silver which it wore about its neck. For a moment it did nothing but grin and stare; then, uttering a discordant scream, it flung into Virginia's lap a filthy piece of carrion, and in an instant it had bounded away with an almost miraculous activity.

Virginia shrieked with disgust and terror, and clung to Paul's knees for protection. He, however, in some strange way, seemed unmoved and preoccupied. All at once, to her intense surprise, she saw his face light up with an expression of triumphant eagerness. 'The missing link!' he exclaimed, 'the missing

link at last! Thank God—I beg pardon
for my unspeakable blasphemy—I mean,
thank circumstances over which I have
no control. I must this instant go out
and hunt for it. Give me some provisions in a knapsack, for I will not come
back till I have caught it.'

This was a fearful blow to Virginia.
She fell at Paul's feet weeping, and besought him in piteous accents that he
would not thus abandon her.

'I must,' said the Professor solemnly,
'for I am going in pursuit of Truth.
To arrive at Truth is man's perfect and
most rapturous happiness. You must
surely know that, even if I have forgotten
to tell it to you. To pursue truth—holy

truth for holy truth's sake—is a more solemn pleasure than even frizzling your hair.'

'Oh,' cried Virginia, hysterically, 'I don't care two straws for truth. What on earth is the good of it?'

'It is its own end,' said the Professor. 'It is its own exceeding great reward. I must be off at once in search of it. Good-bye for the present. Seek truth on your own account, and be unspeakably happy also, because you know that I am seeking it.'

The Professor remained away for three days. For the first two of them Virginia was inconsolable. She wandered about mournfully with her head dejected. She

very often sighed ; she very often uttered
the name of Paul.   At last she surprised
herself by exclaiming aloud to the irre-
sponsive solitude, 'Oh, Paul, until you
were gone, I never knew how passionately
I loved you.'   No sooner were these
words out of her mouth than she stood
still, horror-stricken.   'Alas!' she cried,
'and have I really come to this ?   I am
in a state of deadly sin, and there is no
priest here to confess to!   Alone, alone I
must conquer my forbidden love as I may.
But, ah me, what a guilty thing I am !'

As she uttered these words, her eyes
fell on a tin box of the Professor's, marked
' Private,' which he always kept carefully
locked, and which had before now excited

her curiosity. Suddenly she became conscious of a new impulse. 'I will pursue truth ! 'she exclaimed. 'I will break that box open, and I will see what is inside it. Ah !' she added, as with the aid of the poker she at last wrenched off the padlock. 'Paul may be right, after all. There is more interest in the pursuit of truth than I thought there was.'

The box was full of papers, letters, and diaries, the greater part of which were marked 'Strictly private.' Seeing this, Virginia's appetite for truth became keener than ever. She instantly began her researches. The more she read, the more eager she became; and the more private appeared the nature of the documents, the more insatiable did her thirst for truth grow. To her extreme surprise, she gathered that the Professor had begun life as a clergyman. There were several photographs of him in his surplice; and a number of devout prayers, apparently composed by himself for his own personal use. This discovery was the result of her labours.

'Certainly,' she said, 'it is one of extreme significance. If Paul was a priest once, he must be a priest now. Orders are indelible—at least in the Church of England I know they are.

CHAPTER XV.

PAUL came back, to Virginia's extreme relief, without the missing link. But he was still radiant in spite of his failure; for he had discovered, he said, a place where the creature had apparently slept, and he had collected in a card-paper box a large number of its parasites.

'I am glad,' said Virginia, 'that you have not found the missing link: though as to thinking that we really came from monkeys, of course that is too absurd. Now if you could have brought me a nice monkey, I should really have liked that. The Bishop has promised that I shall have a darling one, if I ever reach him—ah me!—if——Paul,' continued Virginia, in a very solemn voice, after a long pause, 'do you know that whilst you have been away I have been pursuing truth? I rather liked it; and I found it very, very significant.'

'Oh, joy!' exclaimed the Professor. 'Oh, unspeakable radiance! Oh, holy, oh essentially dignified Humanity! it will very soon be perfect! Tell me, Virginia, what truths have you been discovering?'

'One truth about you, Paul,' said

Virginia, very gravely, 'and one truth about me. I burn—oh, I burn to tell them to you!'

The Professor was enraptured to hear that one half of Humanity had been thus studying human nature; and he began asking Virginia if her discoveries belonged to the domain of historical or biological science. Meanwhile Virginia had flung herself on her knees before him, and was exclaiming, in piteous accents—

'By my fault, by my own fault, by my very grievous fault, holy father, I confess to you——'

'Is the woman mad?' cried the Professor, starting up from his seat.

'You are a priest, Paul,' said Virginia; 'that is one of the things I have discovered. I am in a state of deadly sin; that is the other: and I must and will confess to you. Once a priest, always a priest. You cannot get rid of your orders, and you must and shall hear me.'

'I was once in orders, it is true,' said Paul, reluctantly; 'but how did you find out my miserable secret?'

'In my zeal for truth,' said Virginia, 'I broke open your tin box; I read all your letters; I looked at your early photographs; I saw all your beautiful prayers.'

'You broke open my box!' cried

the Professor. 'You read my letters and
my private papers! Oh, horrible! oh,
immoral! What shall we do if one half
of Humanity has no feeling of honour?

'Oh!' said Virginia, 'it was all for
the love of truth—of solemn and holy
truth. I sacrificed every other feeling
for that. But I have not told you my
truth yet; and I am determined you
shall hear it, or I must still remain in
my sins. Paul, I am a married woman;
and I discover, in spite of that, that I
have fallen in love with you. My husband, it is true, is far away; and whatever we do, he could never possibly be
the wiser. But I am in a state of
mortal sin, nevertheless; and I would

give anything in the world if you would only kiss me.'

'Woman!' exclaimed Paul, aghast with fright and horror, 'do you dare to abuse truth, by turning it to such base purposes?'

'Oh, you are so clever,' Virginia went on, 'and when the ends of your moustaches are waxed, you look positively handsome; and I love you so deeply and so tenderly, that I shall certainly go to hell if you do not give me absolution.'

At this the Professor jumped up, and, staring very hard at Virginia, asked her if, after all that he had said on the ship, she really believed in such exploded fallacies as hell, God, and priest-craft.

She reminded him that he had preached there without a surplice, and that she had therefore not thought it right to listen to a word he said.

'Ah!' cried the Professor, with a sigh of intense relief, 'I see it all now. How can Humanity ever be unspeakably holy so long as one half of it grovels in dreams of an unspeakably holy God? As Mr. Frederic Harrison truly says, a want of faith in "the essential dignity of man is one of the surest marks of the enervating influence of this dream of a celestial glory."' The Professor accordingly re-delivered to Virginia the entire substance of his lectures in the ship. He fully impressed on her that all the intellect of the world was on the side of Humanity; and that God's existence could be disproved with a box of chemicals. He was agreeably surprised at finding her not at all unwilling to be convinced, and extremely unexacting in her demands for proof. In a few days she had not a remnant of superstition left. 'At last!' exclaimed the Professor; 'it has come at last Unspeakable happiness will surely begin now.'

CHAPTER XVI.

NO one now could possibly be more emancipated than Virginia. She tittered all day long, and whenever the Professor asked her why, she always told him she was thinking of 'an intelligent First Cause,' a conception which she said 'was really quite killing.' But when her first burst of intellectual excitement was over, she became more serious. ' All thought, Paul,' she said, ' is valuable mainly because it leads to action. Come, my love, my dove, my beauty, and let us kiss each other all daylong. Let us enjoy the charming license which exact thought shows us we shall never be punished for.'

This was a result of freedom that the Professor had never bargained for. He could not understand it, 'because,' he argued, 'if people were to reason in that way, morality would at once cease to be possible.' But he had seen so much of the world lately, that he soon recovered himself, and recollecting that immorality was only ignorance, he began to show Virginia where her error lay— her one remaining error. 'I perceive,' he said, 'that you are ignorant of one

of the greatest triumphs of exact thought
—the distinction it has established between the lower and the higher pleasures.
Philosophers, who have thought the whole
thing over in their studies, have become
sure that as soon as the latter are
presented to men they will at once leave
all and follow them.'

'They must be very nice pleasures,'
said Virginia, 'if they would make me
leave kissing you for the sake of them.'

'They *are* nice,' said the Professor.
'They are the pleasures of the imagina-
.tion, the intellect, and the glorious apprehension of truth. Compared with
these, kissing me would be quite insipid.
Remain here for a moment, whilst I go

to fetch something, and you shall then
begin to taste them.'

In a few moments Paul came back
again, and found Virginia in a state of
intense expectancy.

'Now—,' he exclaimed triumphantly.

'Now—,' exclaimed Virginia, with a
beating heart.

The Professor put his hand in his
pocket, and drew slowly forth from it
an object which Virginia knew well.
It reminded her of the most innocent
period of her life ; but she hated the
very sight of it none the less. It was
a Colenso's Arithmetic.

'Come,' said the Professor, 'no
truths are so pure and necessary as

those of mathematics ; you shall at once
begin the glorious apprehension of them.'

'Oh, Paul,' cried Virginia, in an
agony, 'but I really don't care for truth
at all; and you know that when I broke
your tin box open and read your private
letters in my search for it, you were
very angry with me.'

'Ah !' said Paul, holding up his finger,
'but those were not necessary truths.
Truths about human action and character
are not necessary truths ; therefore men
of science care nothing about them,
and they have no place in scientific systems of ethics.   Pure truths are of a
very different character; and, however
much you may misunderstand your own

inclinations, you can really care for nothing
so much as doing a few sums. I will
set you some very easy ones to begin
with, and you shall do them by yourself,
whilst I magnify in the next room the
parasites of the missing link.'

Virginia saw that there was no help
for it. She did her sums by herself the
whole morning, which, as at school she
had been very good at arithmetic, was
not a hard task for her, and Paul mag-
nified parasites in the next room, and
prepared slides for his microscope.

When they met again, Paul began
skipping and dancing, as if he had gone
quite out of his senses, and every now
and then between the skips he gave a

sepulchral groan. Virginia asked him in astonishment what on earth was the matter with him.

'Matter!' he exclaimed. 'Why, Humanity is at last perfect! All the evils of existence are removed; we neither of us believe in a God or a celestial future; and we are both in full enjoyment of the higher pleasures and the apprehension of scientific truth. And therefore I skip because Humanity is so unspeakably happy, and I groan because it is so unspeakably solemn.'

'Alas! alas!' cried Virginia, 'and would not you like to kiss me?'

'No,' said the Professor, sternly; 'and you would not like me to kiss you. It is impossible that one half of Humanity should prefer the pleasure of unlawful love to the pleasure of finding out scientific truths.'

'But,' pleaded Virginia, 'cannot we enjoy both ?'

'No,' said the Professor, 'for if I began to kiss you I should soon not care two straws about the parasites of the missing link.'

'Well,' said Virginia, 'it is nice of you to say that; but still——Ah me! Ah me!'

And her bosom heaved slowly with a soft, long sigh.

CHAPTER XVII.

VIRGINIA was preparing, with a rueful face, to resume her enjoyment of the higher pleasures, when a horrible smell, like that of an open drain, was suddenly blown in through the window.

Virginia stopped her nose with her handkerchief. The Professor's conduct was very different.

'Oh, rapture!' he cried, jumping up

from his seat, 'I smell the missing link.'
And in another instant he was gone.

'Well,' said Virginia, 'here is one
comfort. Whilst Paul is away I shall
be relieved from the higher pleasures.
Alas!' she cried, as she flung herself
down on the sofa, 'he is so nice-looking,
and such an enlightened thinker. But it
is plain he has never loved, or else very
certainly he would love again.'

Paul returned in about a couple of
hours, again unsuccessful in his search.

'Ah!' cried Virginia, 'I am so glad
you have not caught the creature!'

'Glad!' echoed the Professor, 'glad!
Do you know that till I have caught the
missing link the cause of glorious truth

will suffer grievously ?   The missing link is the token of the solemn fact of our origin from inorganic matter.   I did but catch one blessed glimpse of him.   He had certainly a silver band about his neck.   He was about three feet high. He was rolling in a lump of carrion. It is through him that we are related to the stars—the holy, the glorious stars, about which we know so little.'

'Bother the stars!' said Virginia; 'I couldn't bear, Paul, that anything should come between you and me.   I have been thinking of you and longing for you the whole time you have been away.'

'What!' cried Paul, 'and how have

you been able to forego the pleasures of the intellect ? '

' I have deserted them,' cried Virginia, ' for the pleasures of the imagination, which I gathered from you were also very ennobling. And I found they were so ; for I have been imagining that you loved me. Why is the reality less ennobling than the imagination ? Paul, you shall love me ; I will force you to love me. It will make us both so happy : we shall never go to hell for it ; and it cannot possibly cause the slightest scandal.'

The Professor was more bewildered than ever by these appeals. He wondered how Humanity would ever get on if one half of it cared nothing for pure truth, and persisted in following the vulgar impulses that had been the most distinguishing feature of its benighted past—that is to say, those ages of its existence of which any record has been preserved for us. Luckily, however, Virginia came to his assistance.

'I think I know, Paul,' she said, 'why I do not care as I should do for the intellectual pleasures. We have both been seeking them by ourselves; and we have been therefore egoistic hedonists. It is quite true, as you say, that selfishness is a despicable thing. Let me,' she went on, sitting down beside him, 'look through your microscope along with you.

I think perhaps, if we shared the pleasure, the missing link's parasites might have some interest for me.'

The Professor was overjoyed at this proposal. The two sat down side by side, and tried their best to look simultaneously through the eye-piece of the microscope. Virginia in a moment expressed herself much satisfied. It is true they saw nothing; but their cheeks touched. The Professor too seemed contented, and said they should both be in a state of rapture when they had got the right focus. At last Virginia whispered, with a soft smile—

'Suppose we put that nasty microscope aside; it is only in the way. And then, oh, Paul; dear love, dove of a Paul! we can kiss each other to our heart's content.'

Paul thought Virginia quite incorrigible, and rushed headlong out of the room.

CHAPTER XVIII.

'ALAS!' cried Paul, 'what can be done to convince one half of Humanity that it is really devoted to the higher pleasures and does not care for the lower—at least nothing to speak of?' The poor man was in a state of dreadful perplexity, and felt well-nigh distracted. At last a light broke in on him. He remembered that as one of his most revered masters, Professor Tyndall, had admitted, a great part of

Humanity would always need a religion, and that Virginia now had none. He at once rushed back to her. 'Ah!' he exclaimed, 'all is explained now. You cannot be in love with me, for that would be unlawful passion. Unlawful passion is unreasonable, and unreasonable passion would quite upset a system of pure reason, which is what exact thought shows us is soon going to govern the world. No! the emotions that you fancy are directed to me are in reality cosmic emotion—in other words, are the reasonable religion of the future. I must now initiate you in its solemn and unspeakably significant worship.'

'Religion!' exclaimed Virginia, not

knowing whether to laugh or cry. 'It is not kind of you to be making fun of me. There is no God, no soul, and no supernatural order, and above all there is no hell. How then can you talk to me about religion ?'

'You,' replied Paul, 'are associating religion with theology, as indeed the world hitherto always has done. But those two things, as Professor Huxley well observes, have absolutely nothing to do with each other. " It may be," says that great teacher, " that the object of a man's religion is an ideal of sensual enjoyment, or——" '

'Ah !' cried Virginia, 'that is my religion, Paul.'

'Nonsense!' replied Paul; 'that cannot be the religion of half Humanity, else high, holy, solemn, awful morality would never be able to stand on its own basis. See, the night has fallen, the glorious moon has arisen, the stupendous stars are sparkling in the firmament. Come down with me to the sea-shore, where we may be face to face with nature, and I will show you then what true religion—what true worship is.'

The two went out together. They stood on the smooth sands, which glittered white and silvery in the dazzling moonlight. All was hushed. The gentle murmur of the trees, and the soft splash of the sea, seemed only to make the silence audible. The Professor paused close beside Virginia, and took her hand. Virginia liked that, and thought that religion without theology was not perhaps so bad after all. Meanwhile Paul had fixed his eyes on the moon. Then, in a voice almost broken with emotion, he whispered, 'The prayer of the man of science, it has been said, must be for the most part of the silent sort. He who said that was wrong. It need not be silent; it need only be inarticulate. I have discovered an audible and a reasonable liturgy which will give utterance to the full to the religion of exact thought. Let us both join our voices, and let us croon at the moon.'

The Professor at once began a long, low howling. Virginia joined him, until she was out of breath.

'Oh, Paul,' she said at last, 'is this more rational than the Lord's Prayer ? '

'Yes,' said the Professor, 'for we can analyse and comprehend that; but true religious feeling, as Professor Tyndall tells us, we can neither analyse nor comprehend. See how big nature is, and how little—ah, how little!—we know about it. Is it not solemn, and sublime, and awful ? Come let us howl again.'

The Professor's devotional fervour grew every moment. At last he put his hand to his mouth, and began hooting like an owl, till it seemed that all

the island echoed to him. The louder
Paul hooted and howled, the more near
did he draw to Virginia.

'Ah!' he said, as he put his arm
about her waist, 'it is in solemn moments like this that the solidarity of
mankind becomes apparent.'

Virginia, during the last few moments, had stuck her fingers in her ears.
She now took them out, and, throwing
her arms round Paul's neck, tried, with
her cheek on his shoulder, to make
another little hoot; but the sound her
lips formed was much more like a kiss.
The power of religion was at last too
much for Paul.

'For the sake of cosmic emotion,'

he exclaimed, 'O other half of Humanity, and for the sake of rational religion, both of which are showing themselves under quite a new light to me, I will kiss you.'

The Professor was bending down his face over her, when, as if by magic, he started, stopped, and remained as one petrified. Amidst the sharp silence, there rang a human shout from the rocks.

'Oh!' shrieked Virginia, falling on her knees, 'it is a miracle! it is a miracle! And I know—merciful heavens —I know the meaning of it. God is angry with us for pretending that we do not believe on Him.'

The Professor was as white as a sheet; but he struggled with his perturbation manfully.

'It is not a miracle,' he cried, 'but an hallucination. It is an axiom with exact thinkers that all proofs of the miraculous are hallucinations.'

'See,' shrieked Virginia again, 'they are coming, they are coming. Do not you see them?'

Paul looked, and there sure enough, were two figures, a male and a female, advancing slowly towards them, across the moonlit sand.

'It is nothing,' cried Paul; 'it cannot possibly be anything. I protest, in the name of science, that it is an optical delusion.'

Suddenly the female figure exclaimed, 'Thank God, it is he!'

In another moment the male figure exclaimed, 'Thank God, it is she!'

'My husband!' gasped Virginia.

'My wife!' replied the bishop, for it was none other than he. 'Welcome to Chasuble Island. By the blessing of God it is on your own home you have been wrecked, and you have been living in the very house that I had intended to prepare for you. Providentially, too, Professor Darnley's wife has called here, in her search for her husband, who has overstayed his time.

See, my love, my dove, my beauty, here is the monkey I promised you as a pet, which broke loose a few days ago, and which I was in the act of looking for when your joint cries attracted us, and we found you.'

A yell of delight here broke from the Professor. The eyes of the others were turned on him, and he was seen embracing wildly a monkey which the bishop led by a chain. 'The missing link!' he exclaimed, 'the missing link!'

'Nonsense!' cried the sharp tones of a lady with a green gown and grey corkscrew curls. 'It is nothing but a monkey that the good bishop has been trying to tame for his wife. Don't you see her name engraved on the collar?'

The shrill accents acted like a charm upon Paul. He sprang away from the creature that he had been just caressing. He gazed for a moment on Virginia's lovely form, her exquisite toilette, and her melting eyes. Then he turned wildly to the green gown and the grey corkscrew curls. Sorrow and superstition, he felt, were again invading Humanity. 'Alas!' he exclaimed at last, 'I do now indeed believe in hell.'

'And I,' cried Virginia, with much greater tact, and rushing into the arms of her bishop, 'once more believe in heaven.'

NOTES

'WE now find it (*the earth*) not only swathed by an atmosphere, and covered by a sea, but also crowded with living things. The question is, how were they introduced? . . . The conclusion of science would undoubtedly be, that the molten earth contained within it elements of life, which grouped themselves into their present forms as the planet cooled. The difficulty and reluctance encountered by this conception arise *solely* from the fact that the theologic conception obtained a prior footing in the human mind. . . . Were not man's origin implicated, we should accept without a murmur the derivation of animal and vegetable life from what we call inorganic nature. The conclusion of pure intellect points this way, and no other.' PROFESSOR TYNDALL.

'Is this egg (*from which the human being springs*) matter? I hold it to be so, as much as the seed of a

fern or of an oak.   Nine months go to the making of
it into a man.   Are the additions made during this
period of gestation drawn from matter?   I think so,
undoubtedly.   If there be anything besides matter in
the egg, or in the infant subsequently slumbering in
the womb, what is it?'   PROFESSOR TYNDALL.

'Matter I define as the mysterious thing by which
all this is accomplished.'   PROFESSOR TYNDALL.

'I do not think that the materialist is entitled to
say that his molecular groupings and motions explain
everything.   In reality, they *explain* nothing.'

PROFESSOR TYNDALL.

'Who shall exaggerate the deadly influence on
personal morality of those theologies which have represented the Deity . . . as a sort of pedantic drill-
sergeant of mankind, to whom no valour, no long-
tried loyalty, could atone for the misplacement of a
button of the uniform, or the misunderstanding of a
paragraph of the "regulations and instructions"?'

PROFESSOR HUXLEY.

'(*To the Jesuit imagination*) God is obviously a large individual, who holds the leading-strings of the universe, and orders its steps from a position outside it all. . . . According to it (*this notion*) the Power whom Goethe does not dare to name, and whom Gassendi and Clark Maxwell present to us under the guise of a manufacturer of atoms, turns out annually, for England and Wales alone, a quarter of a million of new souls. Taken in connection with the dictum of Mr. Carlyle, that this annual increment to our population are " mostly fools," but little profit to the human heart seems derivable from this mode of regarding the divine operations. . . . In the presence of this mystery (*the mystery of life*) the notion of an atomic manufacturer and artificer of souls, raises the doubt whether those who entertain it were ever really penetrated by the solemnity of the problem for which they offer such a solution.'

PROFESSOR TYNDALL.

'I look forward, however, to a time when the strength, insight, and elevation which now visit us in mere hints and glimpses, during moments of clearness and vigour, shall be the stable and permanent possession of purer and mightier minds than ours— purer and mightier, partly because of their deeper knowledge of matter, and their more faithful conformity to its laws.'   PROFESSOR TYNDALL.

'The world, as it is, is growing daily dimmer before my eyes. The world, as it is to be, is ever growing brighter.'   HARRIET MARTINEAU.

'. . . When you and I, like streaks of morning cloud, shall have melted into the infinite azure of the past.'   PROFESSOR TYNDALL.

'We, too, turn our thoughts to that which is behind the veil. We strive to pierce its secret with eyes, we trust, as eager and as fearless, and even, it may be, more patient in searching for realities behind the gloom. That which shall come *after* is no less solemn to us than to you.'

MR. FREDERIC HARRISON.

'Theological hypotheses of a new and heterogeneous existence have deadened our interest in the realities, the grandeur, and the perpetuity of an earthly life.'   MR. FREDERIC HARRISON.

'As we read the calm and humane words of Condorcet, on the very edge of his yawning grave, we learn, from the conviction of posthumous activity (not posthumous fame), how the consciousness of a living incorporation with the glorious future of his race, can give a patience and happiness equal to that of any martyr of theology. . . . Once make it (*i.e.* "this sense of posthumous participation in the life of our fellows") the basis of philosophy, the standard of right and wrong, and the centre of a religion, and this (*the conversion of the masses*) will prove, perhaps, an easier task than that of teaching Greeks and Romans, Syrians and Moors, to look forward to a life of ceaseless psalmody in an immaterial heaven.'

Mr. Frederic Harrison.

'We make the future life, in the truest sense, social, inasmuch as our future is simply an active existence prolonged by society; and our future life rests not in any vague yearning, of which we have as little evidence as we have definite conception : it rests on a perfectly certain truth . . . that the actions, feelings, thoughts, of each one of us, do marvellously influence and mould each other. . . . Can we conceive a more potent stimulus to rectitude, to daily and hourly striving after a true life, than this ever-present sense that we are indeed immortal ; not that we have an immortal something within us—but that in very truth we ourselves, our thinking, feeling, acting personalities, are immortal ? '

MR. FREDERIC HARRISON.

'As we *live for others* in life, so we *live in others* after death. . . . How deeply does such a belief as this bring home to each moment of life the mysterious perpetuity of ourselves ! For good, for evil, we cannot die. We cannot shake ourselves free from this eternity of our faculties.' MR. FREDERIC HARRISON.

'We cannot even say that we shall continue to love ; but we know that we shall be loved.'

MR. FREDERIC HARRISON.

'It is only when an earthly future is the fulfilment of a worthy earthly life, that we can see the majesty, as well as the glory, of the world beyond the grave ; and then only will it fulfil its moral and religious purpose as the great guide of human conduct.'

MR. FREDERIC HARRISON.

'I am confident that a brighter day is coming for future generations.' HARRIET MARTINEAU.

'The humblest life that ever turned a sod sends a wave—no, more than a wave, a life—through the ever-growing harmony of human society.'

MR. FREDERIC HARRISON.

'Not a single nature, in its entirety, but leaves its influence for good or for evil. *As a fact, the good prevail.*' MR. FREDERIC HARRISON.

'To our friends and loved ones we shall give the most worthy honour and tribute if we never say nor remember that they are dead, but, contrariwise, that they have lived ; that hereby the brotherly force and flow of their action and work may be carried over the gulf of death, and made immortal in the true and healthy life which they worthily had and used.'

PROFESSOR CLIFFORD.

'It cannot be doubted that the "spiritual body" of this book (*The Unseen Universe*) will be used to support a belief that the dead are subject either to

the *shame and suffering of a Christian Heaven* and
Hell, or to the degrading service of a modern witch.
From *each* of these *unspeakable profanities* let us hope
and endeavour that the memories of great and worthy
men may be finally relieved.' PROFESSOR CLIFFORD.

'I choose the noble part of Emerson, when, after
various disenchantments, he exclaimed, "I covet
truth." The gladness of true heroism visits the heart
of him who is really competent to say this.'

PROFESSOR TYNDALL.

'The highest, as it is the only, content is to be
attained, not by grovelling in the rank and steaming
valleys of sense, but by continually striving towards
those high peaks, when, resting in eternal calm,
reason discerns the undefined but bright ideal of the
highest good—"a cloud by day, a pillar of fire by
night."' PROFESSOR HUXLEY.

'If it can be shown by observation and experiment, that theft, murder, and adultery, do not tend to
diminish the happiness of society, then, in the absence
of any but natural knowledge, they are not social
immoralities.' PROFESSOR HUXLEY.

'For my own part, I do not for one moment admit that morality is not strong enough to hold its own.' PROFESSOR HUXLEY.

'I object to the very general use of the terms religion and theology, as if they were synonymous, or *indeed had anything whatever to do with one another.* . . . Religion is an affair of the affections. It may be that the object of a man's religion—the ideal which he worships—is an ideal of sensual enjoyment.'

PROFESSOR HUXLEY.

'In his hour of health . . . when the pause of reflection has set in, the scientific investigator finds himself overshadowed with the same awe. It associates him with a power which gives fulness and tone to his existence, but which he can neither analyse nor comprehend.' PROFESSOR TYNDALL.

' He will see what drivellers even men of strenuous intellects may become, though exclusively dwelling and dealing with theological chimeras.

PROFESSOR TYNDALL.

‘The two kinds of cosmic emotion run together and become one. The microcosm is viewed only in relation to human action ; nature is presented to the emotions as the guide and teacher of humanity. And the microcosm is viewed only as tending to complete correspondence with the external ; human conduct is subject for reverence only in so far as it is consonant to the demiurgic law, in harmony with the teaching of divine Nature.’ PROFESSOR CLIFFORD.

‘The world will have religion of some kind, even though it should fly for it to the intellectual whoredom of “ spiritualism.” ’ PROFESSOR TYNDALL.

‘All positive methods of treating man, of a comprehensive kind, adopt to the full all that has ever been said about the dignity of man’s moral and spiritual life. . . . I do not confine my language to the philosophy or religion of Comte ; for the same conception of man is common to many philosophies and many religions.’ MR. FREDERIC HARRISON.

SUPPLEMENTARY NOTES

[ii]   The epigraph is taken from Frederic Harrison, "A Modern 'Symposium': The Soul and Future Life," *Nineteenth Century* 2 (1877), 527. The original passage reads: ". . . dignity of man and the steady development of his race, is one of the surest marks . . . ."

[xl]   The epigraphs are from W. K. Clifford, "Cosmic Emotion," *Nineteenth Century* 2 (1877), 429, and from Algernon Charles Swinburne, "Hymn of Man," ll. 198–200 (altered slightly).

52   Rhoda Broughton (1840–1920): A popular sentimental novelist whose early work included *Cometh Up as a Flower* (1867); *Not Wisely But Too Well* (1867); *Good-bye, Sweetheart* (1872); *Nancy* (1873); and *Joan* (1876).

111   Colenso's Arithmetic: A widely used school
            treatise published in 1843 by John William
            Colenso (1814–1883), later bishop of Natal
            and author of many volumes of controver-
            sial Biblical criticism.

[135]   "We now find it . . . this way, and no
            other." John Tyndall, " 'Materialism' and
            its Opponents," *Fortnightly Review* 24
            (1875), 596–597. The emphasis of "solely" is
            Mallock's.

[135]   "Is this egg . . . what is it?" Ibid., p. 598.

136   "Matter I define . . . all this is accom-
            plished." Ibid.

136   "I do not think . . . they explain nothing."
            Ibid., p. 588.

136   "Who shall exaggerate . . . the 'regulations
            and instructions'?" Thomas Henry Huxley,
            "A Modern 'Symposium': The Influence
            upon Morality of a Decline in Religious
            Belief," *Nineteenth Century* 1 (1877), 538.

137   "(To the Jesuit imagination) . . . such a solution." Tyndall, " 'Materialism' and its Opponents," p. 598.

137–138   "I look forward . . . to its laws." Ibid., p. 599.

138   "The world . . . ever growing brighter." Harriet Martineau, *Autobiography*, ed. Maria Weston Chapman (2 vols.; Boston: James R. Osgood and Co., 1877), II, 124. The original passage reads: "The world as it is is growing somewhat dim before my eyes; but the world as it is to be looks brighter every day." This and the following passage from the *Autobiography* had been quoted by W. R. Greg in "Harriet Martineau," *Nineteenth Century* 2 (1877), 112.

138   ". . . When you and I . . . azure of the past." John Tyndall, "The Belfast Address," *Fragments of Science* (2 vols.; New York: D. Appleton and Co., 1896), II, 201.

138   "We, too, turn our thoughts . . . than to

you." Frederic Harrison, "The Soul and Future Life," *Nineteenth Century* 1 (1877), 623.

138 "Theological hypotheses . . . an earthly life." Ibid., p. 838 (altered slightly).

139 "As we read . . . an immaterial heaven." Ibid. Among the slight alterations in Mallock's version, "living incorporation" replaces Harrison's "coming incorporation."

139–140 "We make . . . are immortal?" Ibid., p. 839. In the original the first sentence reads: "We make the future hope . . . ."

140 "As we *live for others* . . . eternity of our faculties." Ibid.

140 "We cannot even say . . . shall be loved." Ibid.

140 "It is only when . . . of human conduct." Ibid., p. 842.

141 "I am confident . . . future generations." Martineau, *Autobiography*, II, 123. The

original passage reads: "that a bright day . . . ."

141   "The humblest life . . . of human society." Harrison, "The Soul and Future Life," p. 837.

141   "Not a single nature . . . *the good prevail.*" Ibid. Italics added by Mallock.

141   "To our friends . . . they worthily had and used." W. K. Clifford, "The Unseen Universe," *Fortnightly Review* 23 (1875), 779–780.

141–142   "It cannot be doubted . . . may be finally relieved." Ibid., pp. 781–782. Italics added by Mallock.

142   "I choose the noble part . . . to say this." Tyndall, " 'Materialism' and its Opponents," p. 587.

142   "The highest, . . . a pillar of fire by night." Thomas Henry Huxley, "Administrative Nihilism," *Fortnightly Review* 16 (1871),

543. The original reads: "The highest, as it is the only permanent, content . . ." and "where, resting in eternal calm . . . ."

142   "If it can be shown . . . social immoralities." Huxley, "A Modern 'Symposium,' " p. 537.

143   "For my own part . . . hold its own." Ibid., p. 539.

143   "I object . . . sensual enjoyment." Ibid., pp. 537–538. Italics added by Mallock.

143   "In his hour . . . neither analyse nor comprehend." Tyndall, " 'Materialism' and Its Opponents," p. 586. Tyndall is quoting James Martineau here.

143   "He will see . . . theological chimeras." Ibid., p. 581.

144   "The two kinds . . . divine Nature." Clifford, "Cosmic Emotion," p. 419. The original reads: "The macrocosm is viewed only in relation to human action . . . ."

144   "The world . . . whoredom of 'spiritual-

ism.' " Tyndall, " 'Materialism' and its Opponents," p. 599.

144   "All positive methods . . . and many
           religions." Harrison, "The Soul and Future
           Life," pp. 634–635.